FRANKIE FOSTER

FREAKS OUT!

Also by Jean Ure

FRANKIE FOSTER

FREAKS OUT!

Here to Help!

Jean Ure

HarperCollins *Children's Books*

First published in Great Britain by HarperCollins *Children's Books* 2012
HarperCollins *Children's Books* is a division of HarperCollins*Publishers* Ltd.
77-85 Fulham Palace Road, Hammersmith, London W6 8JB

The HarperCollins Children's Books website address is
www.harpercollins.co.uk

Jean Ure's website is
www.jeanure.com

1

FRANKIE FOSTER: *Freaks Out!*
Text copyright © Jean Ure 2012

The author asserts the moral right to be identified
as the author of this work.

ISBN 978 0 00 743162-5

MIX
Paper from
responsible sources
FSC® C007454

FSC is a non-profit international organisation established to promote the
responsible management of the world's forests. Products carrying the FSC
label are independently certified to assure consumers that they come
from forests that are managed to meet the social, economic and
ecological needs of present and future generations.

Find out more about HarperCollins and the environment at
www.harpercollins.co.uk/green

All I can say is, it wasn't my fault! I wasn't the one that let Rags in from the garden with muddy paws. I might have been the one that let him out, but I wasn't the one that let him in...

CHAPTER ONE

All I can say is, it wasn't my fault! I wasn't the one that let Rags in from the garden with muddy paws. I might have been the one that let him *out*, but I wasn't the one that let him in. Angel was the one that let him in. It was her responsibility, not mine.

She got all angry when I accused her of it. She said, "He was scraping at the door! What was I supposed to do? Let him ruin Dad's paintwork?"

What she was *supposed* to do was clean up the floor. That is the rule: whoever lets him in with dirty paws has to clean up after him. It wasn't any good her screeching that she was about to go out and was all dressed up. She is always dressed up. She works on the principle that a gorgeous boy could walk into her life at any moment and she has to be prepared. Like she might answer the front door and there he'd be, SuperGuy, and omigod, what a disaster if she was wearing tatty old jeans and a raggedy T-shirt!

Not that she would. She is *obsessed* with the way she looks. Like Mum is obsessed with the kitchen floor.

"Look at my floor!" she goes. "Covered in dog prints!"

It's so weird, the things people get hung up about. My feelings are, a kitchen floor is a kitchen floor. It is *there* to get messed up. But it matters to Mum, and it doesn't do to be small-minded about these things. I could just have left it; I'd have been within my rights. But I was thinking of Mum. Poor Mum! She and Dad work their fingers to the bone taking care of me and Angel and Tom. Well, that is what she always says.

"I don't expect gratitude, but just now and again a bit of consideration wouldn't go amiss."

I think I am quite considerate on the whole. I do like to make Mum happy whenever I can. And I don't mind getting down on my hands and knees, sploshing about on a wet floor. Wouldn't bother me if SuperGuy suddenly appeared.

I filled a bowl with hot water and added a nice big dollop of washing-up liquid. I am one of those people, I believe in doing things properly. I thought while I was there I would give the whole floor a going-over, so when Mum came in she'd be, like, knocked out at the state of it.

"Oh!" she'd go. "Who's cleaned the kitchen floor for me? Whoever it was, they've done an excellent job!"

I crawled all over, getting quite damp in the process. We used to have a mop thingie. A squeegee thing. I used to enjoy using that, but last time I'd used it, it hadn't got put away properly. It had been left propped up against the side of the sink, and Dad had gone and trodden on it. *He* said it was lying on the floor. Don't ask me how it got there. *I* didn't leave it on the floor. But Dad trod on it and snapped it in two and as usual it was my fault. Everything is always my fault. Mum said it was time I learned to put things away after me. But I was going to!

I'd been on the point of shutting the mop back in the cupboard when my telephone rang and there was a text from Jem, something about Daisy Hooper, who is this girl at school that we all absolutely hate, so obviously I had to stop and text back – *Wot u talkin bout?* – and just as I'd done that the phone had gone and rung *again*. It had been Skye this time. I couldn't help it if my friends wanted to talk to me! I got sort of sidetracked and wandered into the garden, talking about Daisy and this super-gigantic row she'd had with her best friend, Cara Thompson, and one thing sort of led to another, cos after speaking to Skye I felt I had to speak to Jem, who is, like, really talkative and practically never stops, plus Rags had come bundling out with me and wanted me to throw his ball, which I had to do cos you can't just ignore him, and by the time I got back it was too late. Dad had gone and trodden on the mop and broken it.

So now we didn't have a mop, which I just bet was the real reason Angel didn't bother clearing up. Catch her down on her hands and knees!

The floor seemed a bit slippy when I'd finished. But at least it was *clean*. Quite sparkling, really. I reckoned Mum would be well happy. I ever so carefully emptied the water down the sink and wrung out the cloth, the way she likes it. She goes mad if you leave it all soggy and dripping. Another of her weird hang-ups!

I was so pleased with the job I'd done that I decided to sit down and read the local paper while I waited for Mum to appear. She'd only popped over the road, so I knew she wouldn't be long. I really wanted to see her face when she opened the door and all the lovely bright shininess rose up before her!

One of my favourite bits in what Dad calls "the local rag" is the horoscope page with Crystal Ball. That is her real actual name. It says so at the top of the column: *Your Horoscope Read by Crystal Ball*. I think that is so neat! I also think there has to be something in it. Fortune telling and stuff. Crystal is really gifted, she can predict all sorts of things. Like once, for Capricorn, which is Dad's star sign, she said, "A big change could be coming your way," and that very same week Dad shaved off his moustache. And once for Gemini, which is Angel, she said, "Diet plays an important part in your life at the moment." Well! You couldn't get much more accurate than that.

Tom said it didn't count since diet always plays an important part in Angel's life. He also said that Dad's didn't count cos he shaved off his moustache himself.

"Wasn't like it was something that just *happened*."

I said, "Well, it hardly could, could it? A moustache can't just fall off by itself."

"Be more impressive if it had," said Tom; and he sniggered, as if he had said something clever.

The trouble with my brother is that he has no imagination. None whatsoever. He says horoscopes are nothing but piffle and bunk. Dunno where he got those words from, but anyway he is wrong, wrong, wrong! Crystal Ball knows what she is talking about. I proved it that morning, without a shadow of a doubt.

I'd just been reading the horoscope for Taurus, which means bull and is *me*, which Mum says is fitting cos it's a perfect description.

"Like a bull in a china shop! Only have to come through the door for things to start crashing down."

Like I said, I get the blame for everything. But guess what? My horoscope was sympathetic! This is what it said:

Not for the first time, you run the risk of being falsely accused. Try to stay calm. Matters will be resolved.

I couldn't help wondering what I was going to be accused of this time. What had I done? I hadn't done anything! Then Mum came in and slipped on my beautiful sparkly floor and nearly broke her neck, or so she said. She screamed, "Good God, Frankie, what have you been up to? This floor's like a skating rink!"

I felt really hurt. After all my hard work!

"I cleaned it for you," I said.

"Well, I'm sure that's very sweet of you," said Mum, pressing both hands into the small of her back, "but what on earth did you use? Furniture polish?"

I said, "No!" Who'd use furniture polish for cleaning a kitchen floor? That would be just stupid. I told her proudly that I'd used washing-up liquid.

"Like about half a litre of it," said Mum. "Do we still have any left?"

Of course we had some left! What was she on about?

Mum just shook her head, like she was feeling defeated.

"What?" I said. "What have I done?"

It seemed I'd used a bit more than I should have.

"All you need –" Mum said it almost pleadingly – "is just the tiniest, weeniest little drop. If any!"

How was I supposed to know? They don't give you measurements.

"The floor was in a right mess," I said. "There were muddy pawprints *everywhere*."

"Yes, you did a splendid job," said Mum.

Well, I reckoned I had, specially as it shouldn't have been up to me in the first place.

"I wasn't the one that let Rags in," I said. "*She* did. She never cleans up after him."

"Don't worry about it," said Mum. "You'll know better next time."

Pardon me? If this was the way I was going to be treated, there wouldn't be any *next time*.

I watched as Mum grabbed a bunch of kitchen roll and set about drying the floor. I guess it *was* still a bit wet. I thought of saying how we needed a new mop, but decided against it on account of that was yet another thing I'd got the blame for. She'd only start on about me not putting things away. Probably best to change the subject.

"Mum," I said, "what's your star sign? Is it Virgo? I'll read your horoscope... *A very bad accident narrowly averted.*" I wrinkled my nose. "What's that mean?"

Mum said it meant that she could have broken her neck and ended up totally paralysed, while as it was she had merely ricked her back. "Which is quite bad enough."

"So, like, something *nearly* happened, but then it didn't."

"In a manner of speaking," said Mum.

Wow! That was two things Crystal Ball had predicted: me getting falsely accused and Mum almost breaking her neck.

I said, "You know Tom thinks that horoscopes are rubbish? Do you think they're rubbish?"

"Absolutely," said Mum.

"Even when they say things that come true, like about you not having an accident?"

"I did have an accident."

"Yes, but you could have had a really *bad* one."

"Tell me about it!"

"No, but really," I said.

"Really," said Mum, "take it from me, horoscopes are a total nonsense. Completely made up."

"You mean, like, people just invent stuff? Like, what shall I say for Virgo? Oh, I know! *You nearly have a bad accident, but in the end you don't*, sort of thing. And then it just happens to come true, and you and Tom say it's all rubbish."

"Coincidence," said Mum. "It's bound to happen occasionally. Then gullible people like you think it's some kind of magic."

I frowned. "What's gull'ble?"

"Easily taken in," said Mum. "You'd believe any

old nonsense!"

What Mum didn't realise was that Crystal Ball had made *two* correct predictions, not just one. But I didn't bother arguing with her. I have noticed before that when people close their minds there is nothing you can do to convince them. It's like Dad and UFOs.

"Flying saucers?" he says. "Load of claptrap!"

He would still say it was claptrap even if one landed in the back garden and a crowd of aliens got out. Fortunately, I am the sort of person who is always open to new ideas; I think it is the way one develops. If we were all like Mum and Dad, we would still be living in caves.

I tore out the horoscope page and put it in my bag to show Jem and Skye as we walked into school.

"Just no way," I said, "*no way* was it my fault!"

Jem and Skye are my two best mates in all the world, but I have to say they are not always as supportive as they could be. You would think they would automatically be on my side. I mean, that is what mates are for. They are not supposed to jeer and make stupid remarks.

I told them in great detail about Rags coming in from the garden with muddy feet. I told them what the rule was. But when I read out my horoscope, about being falsely accused, they treated it like it was some kind of joke.

Well, Jem did. Skye was more like, "Oh, please!" Skye can be just a little bit superior at times. She said, "Yawn, yawn! What's new? You're always being falsely accused."

"Yeah, right," said Jem. She went off into a peal of idiotic giggles. "Nothing isn't ever her fault!"

Crossly, I said, "It wasn't my job to clean the kitchen floor."

"But whoever *did* clean it," said Jem, "left it soaking wet and nearly broke your mum's neck!"

I said, "*So?* It still doesn't make it my fault. Does it?"

Jem giggled again. Skye just hunched a shoulder. I really didn't know what was wrong with Skye these days. She was behaving very oddly. Not depressed, exactly, but certainly not her usual self. She's never been what you'd call a bouncy sort of person, but just suddenly she'd stopped being fun.

"Anyway," I said, "that's not all. Guess what Crystal Ball wrote for Mum? *A bad accident, narrowly averted.*"

Jem cackled. She sounded like a hen that's just laid a square egg. "Living with you, I should think your mum spends her life having bad accidents narrowly averted!"

I decided to ignore the uncouth cackling.

"Seriously," I said, "it can't just be coincidence that she got it right for both of us. And both on the same day!"

"What's my one?" said Jem. "What's she say for Leo?"

"Leo… *Take action now to start de-cluttering.*"

"Oh!" Jem gave a high-pitched squeal. "Mum told me only yesterday that my bedroom was too cluttered and I really ought to see if I'd got any stuff we could give to charity."

Well. So much for her and her silly giggling.

"I reckon that just about proves it," I said.

"What's she say for Skye? Read what she says for Skye!"

"Sagittarius… *You need to face a fear and conquer it.*"

We turned expectantly to Skye.

"I don't have any fears," said Skye.

"You must have *some*," I said. "Everybody has *some*."

"Well, I don't!" She said it quite angrily. "It's all rubbish! What have I got to be scared of?"

"Spiders?" said Jem.

"I'm not scared of spiders!"

"I know, I know!" I clapped my hands. "Not getting A+ for her maths homework!"

"And for her French homework!"

"And for geography!"

"And for history!"

Now I was going off into giggles myself. Skye is

like the class brain; it would frighten the life out of her if she ever got a B for anything. She once got A− for an essay and it threw her into total depression for a whole week.

"You are such *morons*," she said.

I suppose it is not quite fair to laugh at a person, especially if they are one of your best friends, but all the same I do think people should be able to take a joke now and again. I know I can. I am always being laughed at. It doesn't bother me in the slightest. Even if it does, I don't make a big thing of it.

"Where are you going?" said Jem.

"I'm going to *school*, if that's all right with you." Skye flung it at us over her shoulder. "I want to get there *on time*."

We watched as she went stalking on ahead of us, her legs, long and spindly, clacking to and fro like a pair of animated chopsticks.

"What's her problem?" said Jem.

I shook my head. It is a known fact that Skye doesn't have the hugest sense of humour. Unlike me and Jem, who have been known to giggle ourselves senseless, Skye is a very serious-minded person. But still there was something not right.

I said, "I dunno. In some kind of a mood. Thing is, about horoscopes –" I folded up Crystal Ball and put her back in my bag – "they might just be all made up, but that doesn't mean they're rubbish. Loads of what they say actually does come true."

"This is it," said Jem. "I remember once my auntie was told she was going to have a shake-up in her career, and the very next day she shook a bottle of tomato ketchup and the top flew off and it went everywhere, all over the place, and look what happened!"

"What?" I said. "What happened?"

"She got a new job!"

"What, because of the tomato ketchup?"

"No, cos she went down the job centre."

"Because of the ketchup."

"No. She was going there anyway. The ketchup didn't have anything to do with it."

Excuse me?

"Just that she shook it," said Jem. "Like it said in her horoscope… a shake-up. And then she got a job. See what I mean?"

I nodded slowly. I do sometimes find that I have a bit of difficulty following Jem's train of thought. She has a brain that hops about all over the place.

"My auntie was really miffed about the ketchup," she said. "It went all down her blouse, and she couldn't get it out. You can't, with ketchup. But if it hadn't been for that, she might never have got the job. Least, that's what she told Mum, so I reckon you're right. There's got to be something in it."

That was better. At least I'd got one of them to agree with me.

"Know what?" I said. "We could do horoscopes. We could ask everyone what their star signs are, and then we could make up horoscopes for them, and wait and see if they come true."

Jem liked that idea. I could tell, already, that her brain was whizzing into overdrive, thinking what sort of things she could make up.

"What about Skye?" she said. "Are we going to tell her?"

I said yes, we had to. She was our friend; we didn't do things separately. Besides, it might cheer her up. Stop her being so glumpy.

"Even though she thinks it's rubbish?"

"We'll tell her it's just a game," I said. "After all, it's not like we're really *expecting* things to happen."

CHAPTER TWO

"So long as it *is* only a game," said Skye.

I assured her that it was. "Just a bit of fun!"

"So long as that's all."

"It is. I just *said*."

"Cos I think it's really stupid, when people take this sort of stuff seriously."

I laughed, as if the very idea was absurd. "Whoever would?"

"You'd be surprised," said Skye.

"Well, but sometimes –" Jem jumped in eagerly

– "sometimes they get it right. It's just a question of working out what they mean. It's not always straightforward. Like if your horoscope said *'Beware of big hairy monsters!'* and later that night a bunch of spiders went marching across your bedroom ceiling, well, you mightn't realise that that's what it had meant. You might have been expecting something more, like, a load of big hairy muggers coming along and…" Her voice faltered slightly under Skye's withering gaze. "And mugging you," she said. "Or something."

"You might," agreed Skye, "if you were dumb enough."

"No, honestly," said Jem, "they *can* predict things! Like with my auntie. There was this one time—"

Omigod! She was going to go on about the tomato ketchup again.

"I think we should get started," I said.

"But I want to tell Skye about my auntie! See, her horosc—"

"Later!" It's important, with Jem, to stop her

before she gets going. Preferably as soon as she opens her mouth. Mr Hargreaves, our maths teacher, once said that if uncontrolled babble was an Olympic discipline, Jem could babble for England. *And* get a gold medal. "We don't have time for all that now," I said. "We've got horoscopes to write."

Jem looked at me, hurt. "Just because you've already heard it!"

Just because I didn't want Skye hearing it. Fortunately, Skye came to my rescue.

"No, Frankie's right," she said. "If we don't get started we'll never get anywhere. Everybody pay attention! First we need to get organised."

Jem pulled a face. Normally I'd have pulled one too, and even given an inward *gro-o-an*, cos when Skye starts organising she turns into this really evil dictator type, bossing and bullying and laying down the law, but at least she'd managed to stop Jem going on about her auntie all over again.

If Skye had heard the tale of the tomato ketchup she'd have gone into full boffin mode and started lecturing Jem about being gullible, cos you can just bet *she'd* know what gullible meant. Jem would then have got upset, and then they'd have had words, and then they'd have tried dragging me into it, both of them wanting me to be on their side, like, "Frankie, tell her! *You* heard about my auntie," and "Frankie, for goodness' sake! *You* don't believe in all that rubbish?"

I wouldn't have known what to say. I mean, I did *sort* of believe. Sort of. Just not in the tomato-ketchup story. What we needed was some kind of definite proof, which was exactly the reason I was conducting my experiment. Cos that was what it was, I suddenly realised. Not just a game or a bit of fun, but a proper bony fido experiment. Or whatever the expression was.

"What's that thing you say when you mean something's, like, real?" I said.

"You mean, like, real?" said Skye.

"I mean like bony fido, or whatever it is."

"*Bona fide*. It's Latin," said Skye. God, she's like an

encyclopaedia, that girl! I guess it's cos of her mum and dad both being teachers. Always telling her to find things out and look things up. "*Bona* means good and *fide* means faith, and what's it got to do with anything, anyway? I thought we were going to get started?"

"We are, we are!"

"Then let's work out the ground rules."

"What *ground* rules?" Jem was sitting cross-legged on my bed, cuddling Rags. She was obviously in a bit of a sulk. "What do we want *ground* rules for? Why can't we just make up horoscopes like we said?"

Oh, but it wasn't that simple! Nothing is ever simple, with Skye. First off, she made me Google "Star Signs" on my laptop. Then she told me to write them all down.

"*Neatly.*"

Jem and I exchanged glances. Jem put a finger to her forehead and tapped. I just did what I was told. It seemed easier, somehow.

These are the star signs:

Aries (ram)

Taurus (bull)

Gemini (twins)

Cancer (crab)

Leo (lion)

Virgo (virgin)

Libra (scales)

Scorpio (scorpion)

Sagittarius (archer)

Capricorn (goat)

Aquarius (water carrier)

Pisces (fish)

Now, said Skye, we would cut them up.

Excuse me?

"Cut them up!"

She held out her hand for the scissors. I passed them across. Me and Jem watched without saying anything, as Skye turned my list into a load of shredded strips.

"What we do is take out our *own* star signs – well, go on! Take them!" Meekly, we did so. "Put those to one side. Then fold the others over, so we can't see what they are. Now we do our horoscopes. Four each!"

"You mean –" I said it slowly, trying to fathom the workings of her superior brain – "you mean we won't actually know which star sign we're writing stuff for?"

"Exactly!"

"What's the point of that?" said Jem.

The point, said Skye, was that nobody would be tempted to write nice things for some star signs – like if they knew who the sign belonged to – and nasty things for others.

"Though personally," she added, "I'm only going to write nice things, anyway."

"Why?" Jem said it aggressively. I guess she was still pretty mad at Skye for siding with me and not letting her tell the tomato-ketchup story. Not to mention bossing us around. "If you think it's all rubbish, what's it matter *what* you write?"

"Cos I'd feel awful," said Skye, "if I wrote something nasty and then it actually came true. Even though I'd know it was only coincidence."

I saw Jem's mouth open, and quickly shoved my elbow in her ribs. We didn't have all day. We'd come back to my place after school and Skye and Jem would have to be getting home pretty soon.

"Just write," I said.

These are my four that I did:

An exciting new opportunity will arise. It should be grasped with both hands.

Big changes are coming your way. They will take your life in a different direction.

A treasured possession will be lost, but do not despair. It will turn up.

Be on the lookout: trouble ahead!

"OK, I've finished," I said.

"Me too," said Skye.

Jem was still sitting hunched up like a little gnome, furiously scribbling. Now and again, a giggle would burst out of her.

"I hope you're not being *gross*," said Skye.

"What's it to you if I am?" Jem threw down her pen. "*Now* what d'you want us to do?"

"Cut them into strips," said Skye, "then fold them up and shuffle them about so you don't know which is which."

Jem rolled her eyes.

"Do it!"

"Yes, do it," I said.

"All *right*," said Jem. "I'm doing it!"

Skye said that now we would each take one for ourselves. "I'll take one from Frankie, and Frankie can take one from Jem, and Jem can take one from me… *go*!"

"Can we look?" said Jem. "Well, I'm going to, anyway!"

We all opened our bits of paper. On mine, in Jem's round squiggly handwriting, it said: *Things will happen.* Hm! It didn't make much sense, but at least she hadn't said *bad* things.

I asked Skye which one of mine she'd picked, but she wouldn't tell me. She said, "It's got to be *secret*. Like a secret ballot."

"So what happens to all the rest?" Jem wanted to know.

"We randomly assign them," said Skye.

Jem blinked. "You what?"

"We randomly assign them!"

There was a pause.

"I do wish, just occasionally, she would speak in normal English," said Jem.

Skye made an impatient tutting sound. "It's perfectly simple! What we're left with is nine horoscopes and nine star signs." She laid them out in two rows on the floor. "We're going to staple one horoscope to each star sign." She clicked her fingers. "Stapler!"

"Haven't got one."

"Paper clips!"

"Haven't got any."

Skye breathed heavily, like Mr Hargreaves when

he's about to blow up.

"*Sellotape?*"

"Oh, yes," I said. "I've got some of that."

Just as well! It doesn't do to cross Skye when she's in one of her schoolteacherly moods.

With brisk efficiency, she began picking up horoscopes and picking up star signs, folding them over and sticking them together. Jem immediately began bleating.

"If they're all going to be secret, how are we supposed to know if any of them come true?"

Skye said we would wait till the end of term, and then we would open all the bits of paper and see.

"But we don't know what people's star signs are!"

"We know what our mums' and dads' are."

"I'm talking about people at school. I thought we were supposed to be asking them?"

"You can ask, if you want," said Skye. "No one's stopping you. Honestly, I've never known anyone make such a fuss! It's only a *game*."

"So if it's only a game, why can't we look?"

"Cos even games have rules. There's no point playing, if you don't have rules. I'm going to go now, I promised Mum I'd be back by five. You coming?"

"In a minute," said Jem.

"I've got to go *now*. I'll take these with me." Skye scooped up all the bits of paper, neatly stuck with Sellotape. "Cos I know what you two are like."

"Are you saying we'd *cheat*?" said Jem.

"Well, you would, wouldn't you?" Skye opened her schoolbag and stuffed the bits of paper into one of the inside pockets. "They'll be safe there. *I* won't look."

To be fair to Skye, we knew that she wouldn't. After she'd gone, Jem giggled and said, "D'you want to know what I picked?"

I struggled for a few seconds with my conscience. There wasn't any reason I shouldn't know. Just cos Skye had decided it had to be kept secret. Me and Jem hadn't decided. But it was true that Skye was honourable, and we weren't, so I very nobly said no.

"Better not tell me."

"Don't see why not," said Jem. "What right's she got to dictate?"

None at all, really, except that she was our friend and if she wanted to make up rules – well! That was just Skye. At least she'd joined in.

"Wouldn't be fair to go behind her back," I said.

Jem looked for a minute as if she might go off into a sulk again, but then she gave me this mischievous grin and said, "If I was doing your horoscope now, know what I'd say? I'd say, *Keep an eye on Daisy Hooper.*"

"Why?" I couldn't resist asking.

"See if she gets a clonk on the head!"

"Is she likely to?"

"Well…" Jem cackled. "Someone's going to. Hope it's not you! You didn't pick that one, did you?"

Before I could stop myself I said, "No."

"That's good," said Jem. "Means it could be her!"

Me and Jem watched eagerly the next couple of days, waiting to see if Daisy Hooper would get clonked on the head. See if *anyone* got clonked on the head. Just cos Jem had written it for one of her horoscopes, didn't necessarily mean it was going to happen.

"Skye could be right," I said. And Mum, and Tom. And Dad. "*Could* all just be coincidence."

It wasn't what I wanted to believe, cos I like to think there's stuff going on that's a bit mysterious. But if you're conducting a scientific experiment it's important to keep an open mind. Jem already seemed to have made hers up.

"If it's all just coincidence," she said, "why would anyone bother? There's got to be *something* in it. I mean, look at my auntie! You're not telling me that was just coincidence?"

I didn't wish to talk about Jem's auntie. Rather sternly I said, "We are conducting an *experiment*. We must wait for proof."

"But that is proof!"

"*More* proof."

Jem giggled. "Want to know another one I wrote?

Beware the hairy monsters… I thought I might as well use it. Wonder who got that one? Wasn't you, was it?"

"We're not supposed to be telling," I said.

"Oh, pooh!" Jem tossed her head. "What's it matter?" She danced round me, waggling her fingers. "Big hairy monsters! It *was* you, wasn't it?"

"Not saying."

"It was, it was! You're going to get a bunch of huge enormous spiders marching across the ceiling!"

"Yeah, or I might get mugged by a load of huge hairy muggers. Might end up in hospital. Then what'd you have to say?"

Jem's face fell. She looked at me, suddenly uncertain. "It wasn't really you, was it?"

"Well, if it wasn't," I said, "it's someone else, and then you'll be responsible if it comes true."

Quick as a flash, Jem said, "I'm not saying everything does! Just some things."

In the meantime, we kept our eyes fixed firmly

on Daisy Hooper. I guess I wouldn't have minded if she'd got clonked on the head, but all that happened was she got whacked by a hockey stick. On the ankle, not the head.

Jem tried claiming that was just as good. She said you had to know how to interpret these things – they were never straightforward. Clonk on the head didn't have to mean clonk on the actual *head*, it could just as easily mean clonk on the *top part* of something, such as for instance the top part of the foot, which was, of course, *the ankle*. Well, if you looked at it one way it was. *The ankle* was on top of *the foot*. In other words, it was *the head* of the foot. And Daisy had been clonked on it and was now all bandaged up and hobbling.

We wouldn't normally wish ill upon someone, but Daisy Hooper is *such* a disagreeable person. Really loud and overbearing. And mean. She is so mean! Plus she hates us and we hate her.

Jem was eager to open up all our bits of paper and check whether *clonk on the head* had been matched to Daisy's star sign or someone else's. She said, "I know which sign she is, I asked her, she's Libra! So please can we just look? *Please*, Skye? *Please?*"

But Skye said no. She was very firm about it. The end of term was when we were going to look. Not before.

Jem grumbled to me later that "Skye can be such a bore at times!"

I had to admit she was being a bit more bossy than usual.

"Why do we put up with it?" wondered Jem. "It was our game – we invented it. Then she comes barging in and takes over. I think we should tell her."

"Tell her what?"

"That we've had enough! We want all our bits of paper back, and we'll play the game without her."

"Thing is…" I hesitated.

"What?"

"I wouldn't want to upset her."

"But she's upsetting us!"

"Yes, but she's been really funny just lately. Like there's something on her mind."

"Mm." Jem thought about it. "She has been a bit odd."

"It's no use asking her, you know what she's like."

"*Secretive.*"

She is a very controlled sort of person, is Skye. Unlike me and Jem, who tend to splurge, Skye prefers to keep things to herself. She wouldn't dream of splurging.

"What we've *not* got to do," I said, "we've not got to nag, cos that'll only make things worse."

"Make her all ratty."

"We'll just have to be patient." Mum is always urging me to be patient. She says patience is a virtue. I don't get it, myself, I don't think it's natural; I mean you want something to happen, you want it to happen *now*. But as I said to Jem, sometimes you just have to wait.

"Yeah, yeah, yeah!" Jem waved a hand. "Wait till she gets over it."

"Or till she feels like telling us."

"Whatever."

"In the meantime," I said, "we can still go on watching, see if anyone gets clonked."

CHAPTER THREE

We watched like hawks all the rest of the week, but nobody got clonked. Nothing, as far as we could see, happened to anybody, though Jem did turn up for school one morning bubbling over with excitement and obviously bursting to tell me something. She made it clear she couldn't do it while Skye was there, cos she kept pointing at Skye behind her back and pulling faces. If Skye hadn't peeled off at the school gates to go and talk to one of the teachers, I really think Jem would have exploded. Her face had gone bright scarlet with the effort of not saying anything.

"Guess what?" she squeaked, before Skye was even properly out of earshot. "Guess what happened?"

I said, "Tell me, tell me!"

"Huge hairy monsters!" Jem announced it in a trumpet-blast of triumph. Heads swung round to look at us.

I said, "Where?"

"In the kitchen," whispered Jem. "All across the floor!"

Wow! Our first bit of evidence. I stared at her in awe. Skye must have stuck the huge hairy monsters horoscope to the star sign that belonged to Jem's mum. So predictions *could* come true!

"I reckon most people would have screamed," said Jem. "I didn't! Not even when it ran across Mum's foot."

I said, "*It?*"

Her eyes slid away.

"What d'you mean *it*?"

I might have known it was too good to be true. When I questioned her more closely I discovered that in fact it had only been *one* hairy monster and it hadn't even been a proper monster, if it came to that, just one tiny little mouse. Jem tried arguing with me, like she always does. She is a very argumentative-type person. She said that as mice went it had been pretty huge, it seemed to her, plus everybody knew that mice didn't come singly.

"They live in *nests*. With *other* mice."

She said there was obviously a whole family of them hiding away somewhere, and that if you stayed and watched, you'd probably see hordes of them come out and run across the floor. I told her rather sharply that in that case she had better be prepared to sit in the kitchen all night, and *maybe*, if lots of mice appeared, and if they were really *big* mice, I might be prepared to put them on my list.

Jem immediately said, "What list?"

I said, "List I'm making of stuff that happens,

ready for when Skye lets us open up and have a look."

"So what's happened so far?" said Jem.

I had to admit nothing, apart from Daisy Hooper getting whacked on the ankle, which I didn't honestly think we could count. Jem said she reckoned I still ought to make a note of it.

"*And* Mum's mouse. Cos these things aren't ever straightforward."

"Yes, but you can't just twist them to mean anything," I said. "They've got to have a *bit* of resemblance to what's written down."

Jem said, "*Clonk* – Daisy. *Monster* – Mum. That's two of mine, and they do have some resemblance! It could be," she said, "that I'm the one with psychic powers. Not everybody has them. How much of what you wrote has come true?"

Loftily I said, "Too early to tell. I'm waiting for proper scientific proof."

I certainly wasn't putting Daisy Hooper's ankle on the list, and I wasn't putting Jem's mum. Jem could argue as much as she liked. An ankle is *not* the same as a head, and one small mouse isn't the same as a horde of huge furry monsters. On the other hand, something very remarkable happened later that day. I got home to find that a leaflet had been pushed through the letterbox. It was there, lying face up on the mat.

TAKE ADVANTAGE OF THIS EXCITING OPPORTUNITY!
GET FIT, HAVE FUN!
SIGN UP NOW FOR ONE MONTH'S FREE TRIAL AT THE
GREENBANK LEISURE CENTRE.

Well. That was more like it! It was exactly what I'd written: *An exciting new opportunity will arise. It should be grasped with both hands.*

If I could just get someone to grasp it… I rushed into the kitchen to show Mum.

"Mum," I cried, "look! You can have a month's free trial at the Greenbank Leisure Centre!"

Mum said, "Oh, Frankie, I don't have time for that.

I'm far too busy."

It's true that Mum *is* quite busy, doing dressmaking and stuff for all her ladies, but I'd have thought a bit of fun and keeping fit would have brightened up her life.

"Not really," said Mum. "I'd sooner put my feet up and have a cup of coffee."

What can you do? I try to be helpful.

I showed the leaflet to Angel, suggesting she might like to grasp the opportunity, but she seemed to think I was insulting her.

"Why should I need it?" she shrieked. "Are you implying I'm fat?"

I said, "No, but it's free."

"So you do it," said Angel.

Next I tried Tom, who just grunted, which is pretty much all he ever does.

"You mean, you don't want to?" I said.

"Gotta be joking," said Tom.

Dad was my last chance. I reminded him what the government had said about us all taking more exercise to stop from getting fat and flabby, but Dad laughed and said he got quite enough exercise watching sport on TV, thank you very much.

Honestly! What a family. An exciting new opportunity and not a single one of them would grasp it. Still, I put it on my list. It was the first real sign we had had. A *proper* sign. Not like Jem and her hairy monsters. After all, you can't blame horoscopes if people are too stupid to follow their advice. I just wish I knew which one of the family it was!

I couldn't make up my mind whether to tell Jem or not. I knew if I did she would only start arguing again about ankles being the same as heads and tiny little mice being huge furry monsters, but, anyway, as it happened, I didn't get the chance. Skye was with us, as usual, as we walked into school, and we were together all the rest of the day.

Skye was in a really glumpish sort of mood. Even in maths, when Mr Hargreaves wanted to know if anyone had the answer to some weird mess he'd scrawled all over the board, she didn't put her hand up. I could tell Mr Hargreaves was surprised, cos Skye always has the answer to everything. Me and Jem exchanged glances over her head. Something was definitely not right.

We discussed it in whispers in the cloakroom at break. Should we ask what the problem was, or should we just go on pretending not to have noticed? We still hadn't reached any decision when Skye came out of a cubicle and wanted to know what we were gossiping about.

"Not gossiping," said Jem.

"So why are you being all furtive?"

I couldn't think of any answer to that. Jem, her brain whizzing into overdrive, said, "Oh! You know," and waved a hand rather vaguely about the empty cloakroom, but Skye didn't pursue the matter. She obviously wasn't that interested.

Last class of the day was drama with Miss Hamilton. Me and Jem adore drama! Whenever we're told to choose partners, we always choose each other. Never Skye! Not if we can avoid it. Drama is one of the few classes Skye is useless at. She can't act to save her life. It's because she can't show her feelings. Me and Jem like nothing better. We are full of feelings! Sometimes, Miss Hamilton says, we overflow. Skye says we swamp. But I think we are just naturally expressive.

Today, Miss Hamilton said, we were going to do improvisation, making up our own short scenes with a partner. Hooray! I love improvisation. Seems to me it's far more fun making up your own words than having to stick to other people's.

"So," said Miss Hamilton, "find yourselves a partner." Me and Jem immediately bagged each other. We didn't even think of Skye. "I want one of you to be unhappy, and the other one has to find out why, and try to comfort her. OK?"

Jem begged me to let her be the unhappy one.

"*Please*, Frankie, *please*!"

I didn't mind. I'm good at comforting. I'm a people person!

We waited impatiently for our turn. I hate having to sit and watch while everyone else gets up and does things. *Specially* when they're not very good at it. Some of them were OK, like Brittany Fern, crying cos her pet goldfish had died. I think that losing your goldfish would be quite upsetting. I know you can't take a goldfish to bed with you or cuddle it, like I can Rags, but I daresay they have their own little fishy ways that you get fond of.

Daisy Hooper was pathetic, as usual. She's another one that can't act; she just thinks she can. She lumped herself into the middle of the floor and started bellowing about how she'd been promised a trip to Disneyland and then at the last minute it had been cancelled, sob sob, boo hoo. Like anyone cared. Hardly in the same class, I would have thought, as losing your goldfish.

Skye did her scene with a girl called Lucy Westwood that hardly ever speaks above a whisper. It was a bit embarrassing, really, what with Skye all wooden and saying how she'd failed this really important exam – oh, disaster! – and Lucy whispering how sorry she was. Well, I think that was what she was whispering; it was hard to tell.

Me and Jem were left till last. Top of the bill! Stars are always on last. Not meaning to boast, but I do think we are more talented than most people in our class. What I couldn't quite understand, as we took the stage – well, the centre of the room, actually – was why a series of tiny little squeaks were coming from Jem, like she'd got the giggles and was fighting to suppress them. This was serious stuff! Jem was supposed to be unhappy and I was going to comfort her. What was there to giggle at?

I was soon to discover. Miss Hamilton said, "All right, you two, off you go!" I felt that she was expecting something really special from me and Jem. I'd already put my face into sympathetic mode, letting my mouth droop and my eyes go all big and swimmy. It's something I've practised in the mirror. I've practised lots of faces in the mirror. Evil ones, soppy ones, scaredy ones. All kinds! You never know when they might come in useful, like if you're going to have a career as an actor. Not that I am, probably, but I like to think that I *could*. If I wanted.

I turned to Jem, who was still making little squeaks, and said, "Oh dear, Jem, you are not looking very happy! Is something the matter?" Instantly, Jem stopped squeaking and burst into loud, heart-rending sobs. *Real* sobs. I don't know how she does that! It's a gift that she has.

I was immediately sympathetic. "What's wrong?" I said. "Tell me what's wrong!"

"It's my great-great-grandmother!" sobbed Jem.

Pardon me? Her great-great-grandmother? Great-*great*-grandmother?

"She died!" Jem's voice came out in a tragic wail. Someone, somewhere, sniggered. It had to be Daisy Hooper. I put an arm round Jem's shoulders and very gently said, "I'm so sorry. How old was she?"

Jem hiccupped. "A hundred and ten!"

Without thinking, I said, "Is that all?"

I wasn't being sarcastic. It was just, like, an

automatic response. But Daisy Hooper sniggered again. I just knew it was her! Frowning, because sniggering was in *such* bad taste, I offered Jem a paper hankie. Well, a pretend one, really, cos I didn't have my bag with me. Jem mimed taking it and dabbing at her eyes.

"Mum says she was still a girl," Jem sniffled miserably into her pretend hankie. "It was all so unexpected!"

This time, other people sniggered. Something was going badly wrong. We weren't supposed to be a comic turn! I decided that it was up to me to pull things together. Soothingly, I stroked Jem's hair.

"Try not to be too upset. After all, she did have a good long life."

"Yes," said Jem, "but that's not all." She hiccupped again, rather wildly. "My great-uncle just died as well!"

Giggles were breaking out like a rash all over the room. I began to feel rather desperate. I don't mind being laughed at when I'm doing something stupid, but I was being *sympathetic*. I was trying to *comfort*.

"Were you very close?" I said.

"Yes!" Jem howled it at me. "He came to my christening. It's the only time I ever saw him, and now I'll never have the chance!"

At this she collapsed totally, her whole body racked with violent sobs. Everybody except me and Miss Hamilton was in fits. Well, and Skye. She wasn't in fits. I could see her sitting stiff and straight on her chair, not even a slight twitch of the lips. Like I said, Skye is not noted for her sense of humour. I, on the other hand, am the first to laugh if anyone tells a joke. Sometimes, if I'm watching television, for instance, and it's a comedy show, I'll laugh so much I'll fall off my chair and roll about on the floor clutching at myself. It really annoys Angel.

"*Overdoing it,*" she says.

Jem was overdoing it. She was making us look stupid! I was quite relieved when Miss Hamilton stepped in and said enough was enough.

"I wasn't really looking for a comedy duo, but

maybe that's your way of dealing with emotions?"

Jem told me afterwards, as we all walked back from school together, her and me and Skye, that she'd got so impatient having to sit there and listen to everyone else, especially Daisy Hooper dirging on about Disneyland, that when it came to our turn she just couldn't stop herself. I grumbled that she might have warned me what she was planning to do, but she said it wasn't planned.

"It just happened!" And then she had the cheek to add, "You must admit, it was funny."

I pursed my lips and stayed silent.

"*Quite* funny? A *little* bit funny? Just the tiniest *teeny* bit funny?"

"If you really want to know –" Skye, who had been marching ahead like she wasn't really with us, suddenly swung round – "it was stupid and childish and totally insensitive!"

With that, she swung back and went striding on, her legs clacking open and shut like a pair of scissors, her shoes clump-clumping as she went.

Me and Jem were like stunned. I was somewhat annoyed with Jem myself. I'd been looking forward to showing off my people skills, being sympathetic and offering comfort, but even I didn't think she deserved to be yelled at.

"What did I do?" Jem sounded bewildered. "I didn't do anything!"

We broke into a trot, racing along behind Skye.

"Hey!" Jem caught hold of Skye's sleeve, trying to slow her down. "Tell me what I did!"

"You know what you did."

"I don't!"

"Well, you ought."

"But I don't!" Poor Jem was looking so dejected I felt I had to stand up for her.

"She was just having a bit of a joke," I said.

"She was being insensitive! Making fun of –" Skye choked – "people dying!"

"Only her great-great-grandmother," I pleaded. "She *was* a hundred and ten."

"So what?" To my horror, there were tears

streaming down Skye's cheeks. I don't think I'd ever, ever seen Skye in tears. Not even when she broke her wrist, back in primary school and was in agony. "Just because someone's old it means there aren't people that love them?"

I said, "No, of course not."

"Then why make a joke of it?"

Sounding somewhat nervous, Jem said, "I didn't mean to upset anyone."

"No, you just didn't think!" Skye swiped the back of her hand angrily across her eyes. "You never do! You say these things without ever bothering to consider other people's feelings."

Jem chewed uncertainly on her bottom lip. I wondered if she was thinking what I was thinking. It had just come to me that Skye's gran, who lived with them, was a very old lady. Skye's mum and dad are quite old, like her dad is practically a senior citizen. Just a short while back Skye's gran had celebrated her ninetieth birthday. She had had a special birthday party, with people coming from all over the world. Skye had been really excited. She had told us proudly that her gran was going to live to be a hundred and get a telegram from the Queen.

Now I was starting to have horrible feelings. From the look on Jem's face, I guessed that she was also having them. Perhaps we should have started having them sooner, when we'd noticed how unhappy Skye was, but it is *so* difficult when one of your closest friends won't confide in you.

Jem was signalling at me furiously. *Do something!*

To be honest, just for a moment, I felt a bit resentful. I mean, why pick on me? *I* wasn't the one that had laughed about my great-great-grandmother dying. But then I looked at Skye and reminded myself that I was a people person. Jem wasn't a people person. She was bubbly and funny, but she didn't always consider other people's feelings.

It had to be up to me.

CHAPTER FOUR

I took a deep breath, and swallowed. Jem waved her hands at me, like *Say something, say something!* I took another breath and did another swallow.

"Um... Skye?" I dabbed rather nervously at her arm. Skye isn't at all a touchy-feely person like me and Jem. If it had been Jem, I'd have put my arm round her properly, like friends should, but you can't do that with Skye, it makes her uncomfortable. "I wish you'd tell us what's wrong!"

Stiffly, she moved away. "Nothing's wrong! Just

leave me alone."

I didn't dare dab at her again. I took another breath and did a little hop and skip to catch her up, but before I could say anything Jem had gone blundering in, *crash bang wallop*, the way that she does.

"If there's nothing wrong," she said, "what are you crying for?"

Skye turned on her fiercely. "I'm not crying!"

"You were just now," said Jem.

"I was not!"

"You were," said Jem. "You—"

I frowned and kicked Jem quite hard on the ankle. Jem said, "Ow!" and looked at me reproachfully. I was sorry if I'd hurt her, but she really can be quite unhelpful at times. It's strange how some people just seem to totally lose their heads in a crisis.

"Thing is," I said, "we are supposed to be *friends*."

"We are friends," muttered Skye.

"Well, but friends tell each other things."

"It's what they're for," said Jem. "Wouldn't be any

point having them otherwise."

"It's not like we're trying to pry. We're just worried about you."

Skye didn't say anything to that, but at least she had stopped marching and slowed down to a more normal pace. I had this feeling that she *wanted* to talk, she just didn't know how to get started. Suppose this was drama with Miss Hamilton? What would I say?

"It's not your gran, is it?" The words burst out of me. "Skye? It's not your gran?"

The tears sprang back into her eyes. She dashed them away ferociously on her sleeve. Timidly I said, "S-Skye?"

So then, at last, she told us. How two weeks ago, her beloved gran had had a stroke and been taken to hospital. How she had died over the weekend.

"She was so brave," said Skye. "She fought so hard! And now she's gone, and I'm going to miss her so much. She was just, like, always there for me, you know? Like if I was worried about anything,

I could always go to her. And that time I was off school for weeks, when I was ill? She was the one that looked after me. She always looked after me! She was the one I went to if I was in trouble, like once when I got this really bad mark for English, like really really bad, and I couldn't tell Mum or Dad, I was just so ashamed, so I told Gran and she made me realise there was more in life than just passing exams, and it sort of cheered me up for a bit, cos I knew she was right, even if Mum and Dad wouldn't probably agree, and now she's not here any more and I don't have anyone to turn to!"

"You have us," I said.

"I know." Skye sniffed, and nodded, and tilted her chin. "I'm sorry I didn't tell you before. I just couldn't bear to talk about it."

But now that she had, she admitted it did make her feel a bit better.

"Talking does help."

"Talking's what you have to do," said Jem. "When Poppy died I talked and talked."

Poppy was a guinea pig that Jem had had at primary school. I could remember her talking. We had all been sympathetic cos, I mean, a guinea pig is like a member of the family, like a cat or a dog. I was a bit concerned, though, in case Skye might think it was wrong to compare her gran to a guinea pig. Anxiously, I said, "Of course, it's not the same."

"I'm not saying it's the same," said Jem. "Just that talking is good."

"It is," said Skye. "And you're right, it's what friends are for. So thanks, you guys!"

We parted company as usual at Sunnybrook Gardens. Skye waved quite cheerfully, and said, "See you tomorrow!" I realised it was the first time she'd done that for ages. She was obviously feeling *lots* better. I was pleased to think it was all because of me – well, and a little bit because of Jem. To be fair to Jem, she had tried. But I was the one who'd got Skye to talk!

I told Mum about it when I got home.

"She's been *so* miserable. But she just wouldn't say anything, you know? She never does."

"I guess she doesn't find it easy," said Mum. "She's not exactly one of nature's chatterboxes. Unlike someone I could name!"

I said, "Mum, are you talking about me?"

"Well, if the cap fits," said Mum.

I thought about it. It's true, I suppose; I do get told off quite a lot for talking, though not nearly as much as Jem. The thing about Jem, it has to be said, she doesn't always stop to think before she opens her mouth. Like this one time when a girl in our class, Amy Shah, was telling us how she was trying to lose weight, saying she didn't want to lose too much, just a tiny little bit, and Jem goes jumping in and says right, cos if she lost too much it would look really silly, a tiny little body with a huge great face on top of it. Daisy Hooper went, "Ooh, nasty!" and Lucy didn't speak to Jem for the whole of the rest of term. Jem never properly understood what she'd done to upset her.

"All I said was she's got a big face and it would look silly!"

Like comparing Skye's gran to a guinea pig. I'd have been well pleased if she'd gone and undone all my good work.

"Anyway," said Mum, "do I take it Skye's feeling better?"

"Loads! Of course, she's still sad."

"She will be," said Mum. "It'll take a while."

I couldn't help wondering how I would feel if it was one of my grans that had died. I sat in the kitchen, trying to imagine it, but the thought of either of them not being there any more was just too upsetting. And *that* was only in my imagination. Plus I only get to see my grans once or twice a year, like at Christmas or on birthdays. Skye's gran had actually lived with her. No wonder Skye had been so down.

I wished, now, that we'd been nicer to her. We'd been so horrid, that day we were writing horoscopes and she'd driven us mad by inventing all these insane rules and ordering us around. We'd kept tutting, and rolling our eyes, and pulling faces behind her back. She must have known we were doing it. I wished we hadn't! But at least now we'd made up for it a bit.

I suddenly became aware that Rags had ambled across the kitchen and laid his big doggy head on my lap. He gazed up at me, full of love. He is such a sweet boy! He always knows if you're feeling a bit low.

Angel came bursting through the door as I was making crooning noises and rubbing my cheek against Rags head.

"What's up with you?" she said. "You in pain or something?"

I said, "Skye's grandma has just died."

"Oh." Angel wandered across to the fridge. "I thought p'raps an elephant had trodden on your foot." She yanked open the fridge door and stood there, peering inside. "Hey, Mum, are we out of yogurt?" she said.

She can be just so insensitive at times. Well, all of the time, really.

"*Mu-u-um!*" She slammed the fridge door shut. "We're out of yogurt!"

"Skye's very upset," I said.

"Yeah?"

"Like anyone would be." Any normal person.

Angel helped herself to an apple and sank her teeth into it. She chewed noisily.

"I thought her gran was ancient. Like about a hundred and three, or something."

"Doesn't mean Skye didn't love her! How'd you feel if one of our grans died?"

"God, do you have to be so morbid?" cried Angel. "They're not going to die! They're nothing like that old."

It was a sort of comfort. In my mind, I'd already been picturing funerals and graveyards. I do tend to get a bit carried away. It's the curse of having an active imagination. I don't think Angel has any at all, which is why she is so insensitive.

Next day, on our way into school, Skye turned to me and said, "Guess what?" The way she said it, my heart sank. Sometimes when people say "Guess what?" it means, "Hey! Guess what? Good news!" Other times it's more like, "Hey, guess what? We're having double maths. Yuck, yuck!" In other words, something bad.

I just knew from the glum tone of Skye's voice that this was one of those other times. *Not* good news. I immediately felt anxious. Skye had seemed so much happier when we'd parted company the previous day. What could have happened to make her all upset again?

Jem, who had been prancing about on the pavement burbling something about her mum trying to force her to eat sprouts (I wasn't really listening), stopped halfway through a sentence with her mouth hanging open. She slid her eyes in my direction.

"You'll never believe it," said Skye.

Obediently, in chorus, me and Jem went, "What?"

"We can't find Gran's pencil!"

For just a minute I couldn't think what she was talking about, and then it came to me. I remembered how, in primary school, Skye had brought in this very special pencil that belonged to her gran, and had belonged to *her* gran before. It was silver, and had been made by Skye's great-great-something-or-other-granddad, over a hundred years ago. Skye had explained that it was a family heirloom.

We'd all had a go writing with it, twisting the lead up and down. Our teacher had said it was what used to be called a propelling pencil, but was now mostly known as an automatic pencil. Skye had told us, with great pride, that her gran was going to leave it to her when she was gone.

"She's going to put it into her will."

And now, it seemed, the pencil had vanished.

"We've searched everywhere! We think maybe she took it out into the garden one day and it dropped out of her bag and she didn't realise."

Jem said, "Why would she take it into the garden?"

"Cos she used to like to sit out there, doing the crossword. And she always used her pencil."

I had a faint memory of Skye's gran sitting in the garden. An old, old lady, very thin and frail, with white hair. A rug round her knees and the newspaper on her lap.

Skye, choking slightly, said her gran hadn't been able to do the crossword for months. Not since last summer.

"She couldn't see well enough. That's why Dad thinks she might not have known she'd lost it."

"That's terrible," said Jem. "If it's silver, it could be valuable."

"Like I should care about *that*?" Skye glared at her. "I don't want to sell it! I just want to *have* it cos it was Gran's, and it would make me think of her."

"Yes." Jem nodded wisely. "I can see that."

"Dad says we'll have a look round the garden, but he doesn't hold out much hope cos we had builders in and they churned everything up. He says it could be buried somewhere."

"Or the builders could have stolen it," said Jem. "I mean," she added, "if it's valuable. They wouldn't care if it had belonged to your gran."

I wasn't quite sure it was right to accuse the builders of stealing. My dad's an electrician. He goes into people's houses all the time to fix things. He wouldn't dream of stealing! Skye didn't seem to think the builders would, either.

"Dad says they could have dumped rubble on it when they built the extension."

"Could always get them to come in and dig it up again," said Jem.

Skye said yes, she could just see her dad doing that. "It's already cost him a fortune!"

Jem looked hurt. "I'm only trying to be helpful."

"I know." Skye thrust her hair back over her ears. "I just thought I'd tell you, that's all. Cos of us being friends and everything? I know there's nothing you can actually do."

"'Cept listen," said Jem.

"Which you have."

"Has it made you feel better?"

Skye said that it had, but I could tell she was only saying it to keep Jem happy. She was really upset about not being able to find her gran's special pencil. I wished there was something I could suggest! I didn't seem to have contributed very much to the conversation. Jem at least had tried.

I worried about it all the rest of the day. Skye had made a real effort. She had opened up to us – well, to *me*, mainly. I was the one she'd turned to – Jem had been too busy burbling about sprouts. Skye had said, "You'll never believe it!" and all I'd managed to say in reply was, "What?"

I have often thought that when I leave school I should like to be someone that helps people. Someone that people can turn to when they are in trouble, like for instance, if their marriages are breaking up. I believe it is something I would be good at. I would not only listen patiently to what they had to say, I would also give practical advice and offer words of comfort. I wouldn't just say *what*?

I felt like I had let Skye down. I really hadn't been any use at all.

At the end of school me and Jem walked home by ourselves, as Skye had a meeting to go to. She is always having meetings. She is our class representative on the school magazine and takes her job very seriously.

"Do you think we helped this morning?" said Jem. "I think we did! Don't you?"

"Dunno." I kicked at an empty can, sending it flying across the pavement and into the gutter. I find there is a lot of satisfaction to be gained from kicking at things.

We watched in silence as a car drove past. Right over the can, squashing it flat. Jem said, "Hm!" And then, "Don't you think so?"

"See, I'm having these horrible feelings," I said.

"'Bout what?"

"That it's all my fault."

"Dunno how you work that out," said Jem. "You didn't have anything to do with it."

"I might have done."

"How?"

"Well, like… if I'm psychic, or something?"

"*You?*"

Jem did this squirrelly thing that she does, bunching up her mouth as if chewing on nuts. I could see she wasn't impressed. *She* was the one that was psychic, or so she thought. Her and her clonks on the head and big furry monsters. I, on the other hand, was serious.

"I'm really worried," I said. "I did this horoscope about losing something precious, and now it's gone and happened!"

"You don't know that for sure. You don't even know if it was the one Skye picked."

"No, but suppose it was?"

"Well, suppose it was," said Jem. "Depends what you wrote. What *did* you write?"

I frowned, trying to remember. "*A treasured possession will be lost, but do not despair. It will turn up.*" I'd been quite proud of it at the time. I thought it read like a real proper horoscope such as Crystal Ball might have done.

"I can't see what you're so fussed about," said Jem. "What's the problem? 'Cording to you, it's going to turn up."

"But I didn't say *when*. It could be months – it could be years!"

And in the meantime, poor Skye was desperately unhappy all over again.

"You still don't know," said Jem, "if it was the one she picked. Even if she did, it doesn't mean you're psychic, necessarily. Could just be coincidence."

"You didn't seem to think it was coincidence when Daisy got clonked on the ankle, or when *one tiny little mouse* ran across your kitchen floor. You even tried saying an ankle was the same as a head!"

"I didn't say it was the *same*. I said it was a head *of sorts*. A *sort of* head. Anyway, you wouldn't let me have it, so why should I let you have yours?"

"We're not in competition," I said.

"That's not the point. You've got to have proof."

"I could always try asking Skye. See if it's the one she got."

"That'd be cheating! Unless you're going to tell me which one you got?"

I said, "The one I got was totally meaningless, if you must know. It was one of yours," I added, in case she had forgotten.

Jem flushed. "If you're going to be insulting—"

"Oh, look," I cried, "don't let's quarrel! We've got to think of Skye and how we can help find her gran's pencil for her."

"Well, if you're so psychic," said Jem, "I don't reckon it should be any problem." She cackled. "Just look in your crystal ball!"

CHAPTER FIVE

While it is true that Jem is one of my very, very, VERY best friends, and I wouldn't want to be disloyal or anything, it has to be said that most of the time she talks absolute twaddle. This is what Mr Hargreaves calls it.

"Twaddle! Absolute twaddle!"

She is quite happy doing it, I don't think she even realises, but it does mean that me and Skye don't always pay very much attention, so that on the rare occasions when she does happen to say something sensible, or come up with a good idea, it tends to get overlooked. It wasn't till ages later, not till the middle of the night, that it suddenly struck me: *Just look in your crystal ball!*

I hadn't taken any notice at the time cos I knew it was just Jem thinking she was being funny. She didn't really believe that I was psychic. But suppose I actually was? I really *might* be able to use my powers to find Skye's missing pencil!

I was so excited I could hardly wait for getting-up time. Mum was quite amazed to find me downstairs in the kitchen, all dressed and ready, without her having to yell at me. I said, "Mum, I know you don't believe in horoscopes, but do you think some people have special powers?"

"How do you mean?" said Mum.

"Well, like when the police call people in to help with murder enquiries, and they go into trances and tell them where the body's buried."

Mum said, "Ah, but do they?"

"They do on television," I said.

"They do a lot of things on television. What's all this sudden interest in the supernatural, anyway?"

"I'm just trying to think of a way to help Skye." I explained to Mum about the special pencil and how nobody could find it. "I was wondering, maybe, if one of us might have psychic powers."

It had to be me, if it was anyone. Jem had shown *no* traces, despite her ramblings about clonks on the head and big furry monsters. As for Skye, she reckoned, like Mum, that it was all nonsense. So *she* couldn't be psychic. Whereas I kind of had this feeling that I might be.

"If I were you," said Mum, "I wouldn't go meddling in that sort of thing."

I pounced, eagerly. "Why not?"

"You never know what it might lead to."

"Might lead to us finding Skye's pencil!"

"Yes, and it might lead to one of you getting disturbed, or frightened."

"But, Mum," I said, "we've got to do *something*. Skye's, like, really upset!"

"In that case, why don't you offer to go and help her have another look? Three pairs of eyes are always better than one."

I said, "She has looked. She's looked everywhere."

"It wouldn't hurt to give it another go. I certainly wouldn't start messing around trying to read tea leaves."

Read tea leaves? What on earth was she talking about?

"It's what people used to do," said Mum. "Back in the days before tea came in tea bags. You'd make a cup of tea and let the tea leaves settle, then you'd try and read things into them."

Aha! This sounded promising.

"What sort of things?"

"The usual stuff. *You will meet a tall, dark stranger*, or *go on a long journey*, or *come into a fortune*... that kind of thing."

I crinkled my nose. I needed to get to the bottom of this!

"How did they do it?"

"Oh, don't ask me! They just called it reading the tea leaves."

"What, like, they spelled out messages?"

"So it was claimed. Something to do with the patterns they made."

I frowned, trying to imagine a crowd of tea leaves in a tea cup. Maybe if they were all bunched together it would mean one thing, and if they were scattered it would mean another. But what?

"Don't worry about it," said Mum. "Nobody took it seriously. Just a few crackpots."

I thought, *Yes, or those with psychic powers...* I wondered if you could do it with tea bags. Like if you tore a tea bag open and put it into a cup, would it make tea leaves?

I suggested it to Mum, and she said, "No, it wouldn't! It would just waste a tea bag. Don't even think about it."

But I couldn't stop thinking about it. I was so excited that I rang Jem.

"We've got to get some tea leaves!" I said.

"What for?" said Jem.

"So we can find out where Skye's pencil is. Does your mum have any?"

"What? Tea leaves?"

What else?

"Dunno," said Jem. "Dunno what they are."

"Things you make tea with!"

"I thought you made it with tea bags," said Jem. And then, before I could explode, cos I did *so* want to get on with it, "Oh, I know!" she cried. "You mean tea out of a packet?"

Yessssss! "Has your mum got any?"

Jem said no, but her nan had. "She says it's the only way you can make a proper cup of tea."

I said, "But your nan lives miles away!"

"You can get it in the supermarket," said Jem. "What d'you want it for?"

I told her what Mum had said, about people reading tea leaves. "I'm going to Google it," I said. "See if I can find out how to do it. Maybe we could buy a packet on the way home tomorrow and give it a try."

"I expect it'll only work if one of us is psychic," said Jem. "But that's all right, cos I think I probably might be."

I ground my teeth and reminded myself that we were doing this for Skye, not for the honour and glory of having psychic powers.

There was loads on the computer about tea-leaf reading. I found five whole pages telling you how to interpret the signs! There was also a page full of how you had to swirl the cup three times clockwise, and what it meant if bubbles came to the surface, and a lot of other stuff I didn't specially want to know about, so I didn't bother with any of that, I just printed out the five pages of signs.

I had to do it in Mum and Dad's bedroom, where Dad keeps his computer and all his business stuff. If Mum had asked me, I'd have said it was homework, but fortunately she was safely shut away downstairs with one of her ladies, taking up a hem or doing a fitting. I had this feeling she wouldn't be happy about me and Jem preparing to read tea leaves.

"Dunno what she's got against it," I said as we called into the corner shop next day on our way home from school to buy a packet of tea. "She seems to think it's messing with the supernatural. We'd better do it round your place, just in case, and maybe best not to tell your mum."

We probably could have told Jem's mum as she isn't at all the sort of person to get fussed, but Jem made up this story about how we wanted to try "real proper tea, like Nan has". Her mum laughed at that. Jem's mum does a lot of laughing. She is big and jolly and what I call a fun person. She said, "You probably won't notice any difference from ordinary tea bags, but you can make me a cup while you're about it."

When we'd made it, she laughed some more cos she said we'd done it wrong.

"You're supposed to pour it through a strainer,

not just dump the tea leaves in the cup!"

We couldn't very well explain that we *wanted* tea leaves in the cup.

"It'll be all right," said Jem. "We'll just let them settle."

We rushed along the hall to Jem's bedroom.

"Now what do we do?" said Jem. "We don't have to *drink* it, do we?"

I said, "Yuck, no!" I hate tea. "We'll just pour it away and leave the tea leaves."

Easier said than done! But we were left with a smattering, more in Jem's cup than in mine, which pleased her as it confirmed her belief that she was the one that was psychic.

I said, "Now all we have to do is read the signs. I'll read mine, and you read yours."

"What are we looking for?" said Jem.

I was tempted to retort that if she was psychic she wouldn't need to ask, but I dug out my list and said, "See if there's anything that looks like one of these."

We both peered intently into our cups.

"I've got a thing like a bow and arrow," said Jem.

I said that I had what looked like a dog.

We rushed to consult the list. Bow and arrow wasn't on it. Dog was! If the tea leaves made the shape of a dog, it meant *good friend*, unless it was at the bottom of the cup, in which case it meant *friend needs help*. Mine was kind of, like, halfway, so "Good friend needs help?" I said.

Jem made a sound like a baby elephant trumpeting. She said it wasn't fair. "You already knew what was on the list!"

I assured her that I didn't. "I didn't have time to read it."

"I bet you had a look!"

I didn't argue with her. I knew she was probably just a bit jealous, cos of bow and arrow not figuring.

"Anyway," she said, "where's it s'posed to have got us? Hasn't got us anywhere! We still don't know where the pencil is."

I said, "No, but at least it's proved one of us has

psychic powers."

I was careful not to say which one, cos I didn't want to upset her. But, I mean, *good friend needs help*. What more proof could you want?

She still went into a huff. "Don't see it proves anything, personally," she said.

I said, "Maybe it does and maybe it doesn't. What we ought to do is try other things."

"Like what?"

"Like… well! Crystal ball, like you said."

I thought that would please her, seeing as it had been her idea, but she just sniffed and said, "Where d'you think you're going to get one of them?"

I said, "I dunno! Make one?"

"Then what?"

"Then we can gaze into it, and if one of us is psychic, we'll see things."

Jem said, "I think it'd make more sense if we asked Saint Anthony."

Pardon me? I tried not to let my mouth gape open. You don't expect Jem to know about saints and all that kind of stuff.

"What would he do?" I said.

"He's the one you pray to for things that have gone missing."

"What, and he tells you where they are?"

"Dunno if he actually *tells* you. Just helps you find them."

"Hm." I was a bit doubtful, cos after all, who was this saint person? I didn't know anything about him! Plus I was really eager to get on with the psychic stuff. Still, if it was what Jem wanted, it seemed only fair to give it a go.

"I s'pose we could try him," I said.

"I could try him," said Jem. "You couldn't, cos you're not a Catholic."

I immediately bristled. "What difference does that make?"

"He's not your saint! He's one of ours."

"Are you saying he only helps Catholics?"

"N-no. Not exactly. Just that he's more likely to listen to me than he is to you."

"Don't see why," I said. "Not as if you ever go to church."

"I used to! When I was little."

"You haven't ever since I've known you. I bet it only works if you go regularly."

"Well, anyway," said Jem. "Nothing to stop me asking him."

"I think you ought to make a promise that if he helps us find the pencil, you'll start going to church. *Regularly.* Like you should," I added.

She didn't care for that. In these quite aggressive tones she said, "Why should I?"

"Cos it's only right," I said. "You can't expect him to do you a favour if you're not offering him something in return. That's the way it works. Like, *Please God, don't let Mr Hargreaves discover I copied my maths homework and I'll never do it again*, sort of thing."

I could see the struggle going on in Jem's head. Pleadingly, she said, "Couldn't I just promise to go, like, every now and again? Like on his saint's day. I could go on his saint's day!"

"*No.*" I was very firm. "If you're going to do it, you've got to do it properly. You have to be prepared to make sacrifices."

"Why me?" said Jem.

"Cos you're the one that suggested it!"

She sulked for a bit, but there wasn't really very much she could say.

"Are we agreed, then?" I said. "You'll promise to go to church *every single Sunday*?"

Jem waved a hand, impatiently. "Yeah, yeah!"

"So, go on, then. Do it!"

"I can't do it *now*," said Jem. "I'll do it when I go to bed."

I imagine that talking to a saint is quite a private sort of thing, so I didn't press her. I said, "OK, so long as you don't forget. I'd better be getting home now, or Mum'll wonder where I am. How long d'you think it'll take?"

"Only a minute or two," said Jem. "I'm not spending all night on it!"

"No, I meant… how long before we know if he's going to help us?"

"I'm not sure." Jem pressed a finger to the tip of her nose, making it go all turned-up and piggy. I don't know why she does that. It's like chewing fingernails, which is another thing she does. "Let's ask Mum! She'll know."

Mrs McClusky was still in the kitchen, mixing something lovely and gooey in a bowl. She is always making lovely gooey things.

Jem said, "Mum, have you ever prayed to Saint Anthony?"

"Ah! Saint Anthony, God bless him. A dear man, to be sure." Mrs McClusky held out a spoon. "Want a bit of splodge?"

We both greedily opened our mouths.

"Did you ever ask him to find anything for you?"

"I did, yes. My purse, with all my cards in it."

Politely, I said, "Did he find it?"

"Well, no, I can't say he did. But I'm sure he tried his best."

I looked rather hard at Jem. *That* wasn't very encouraging.

"Mind you, he did find your auntie's engagement ring for her."

Jem shot me a smug glance. I wondered if this was the famous auntie that had splattered tomato ketchup all over the place.

"How long did it take?" said Jem.

"I can't really remember. A few weeks, I think. She was going spare, and then it turned up somewhere very odd. Somewhere she'd never even thought of looking."

Jem nodded wisely. "He led her there. It's what he does. He leads you to things."

"Well, he'd better lead us to Skye's pencil a bit quicker than he led your auntie to her engagement ring." I said it rather sternly as we parted company at the front door. "We can't wait for ever!"

CHAPTER SIX

"I suppose –" Jem turned hopefully to Skye as we walked into school next morning – "you didn't find your gran's pencil yet?"

Very slowly and sadly, Skye shook her head. I felt so sorry for her. She looked really dejected.

"Not even a hint?"

Skye seemed puzzled. "What sort of a hint?"

"Well, like… a sign, sort of? Like suddenly something tells you to go and look in a certain place, or you suddenly see something and it gives you an idea, or…" Jem's voice petered out. "That sort of thing," she said rather lamely.

"Dad still thinks it got buried when they built the extension. In which case," said Skye, miserably, "it'll be there for ever."

"You don't actually *know* that," I said. "Not for certain."

"It's the only thing we can think of. We've searched and searched all over the place."

"Maybe we should come and help look?" I turned to Jem. "We could do that, couldn't we?"

Jem nodded, brightly.

"After all," I said, "three pairs of eyes are always better than one. What d'you think?"

"S'pose you could, if you wanted," said Skye. "Don't really see that it'll do much good."

She was being a bit ungracious, but I forgave her.

"We'll come back with you after school," I said. "We'll look in your gran's room. We'll look *all over*."

"Yeah. All right." Skye hunched a shoulder, like, *Suit yourself. It'll only be a waste of time.* I knew she couldn't help it; she was still upset at losing her gran. If we could just do something to find her pencil for her, it would make her so happy.

"Who knows? We might be shown a clue," said Jem. "I wouldn't be surprised!" She bounced and swung her bag over her shoulder. "Might just come to us, like… *Look under the carpet*, or – or *Look in the corner*, or—"

Skye gazed at her rather irritably. She'd probably looked under the carpet already. And in the corner.

"Well, I mean, you never know," said Jem. "My auntie thought her engagement ring had gone for ever, but then this voice told her to go and look in this particular place that she'd never looked in before and there it was, after all that time!"

"How long?" said Skye.

"Don't really know. But she got it back!"

"So where was it in the end?"

But of course Jem didn't know that, either. Skye shook her head as we walked in through the school gates. I jabbed at Jem with my elbow.

"Did you do it?" I hissed.

She hissed back at me. "Yes!"

So that was why she thought there might be a sign. I just hoped Saint Anthony had been paying attention when she talked to him.

We went back with Skye after school and Skye told her mum that we were going to have another search of her gran's bedroom.

Her mum said, "I'm afraid you won't find anything, but by all means give it a go."

Skye's mum is as different as can be from Jem's. There is nothing round and jolly about her. She's loads older for a start, almost like *she* might be someone's gran. She is quite nice, but she teaches science and is ferociously clever in a rather forbidding sort of way, which is maybe, I sometimes think, the reason Skye finds it so difficult to talk about her feelings. What I mean is, you can't ever imagine her and her mum settling down to a cosy chat, like I can with my mum.

She asked us, as we prepared to troop upstairs, if

we'd be staying to tea. If it had been Jem's mum we would have said yes please, and we'd all have got together in the kitchen and just grubbed around.

"Help yourselves! Go look in the cupboard, see what you fancy."

That's what Jem's mum would have said. But we knew with Skye's mum it would have meant the table being properly laid, with knives and plates and cups and saucers, so we very politely said no, thank you, we had to get home.

"This is Gran's room."

Skye flung open a door and we walked into this really sad, empty space. The bed was stripped and all the surfaces were bare. Me and Jem gazed round helplessly, waiting for a sign, but none came. Skye watched as we made a show of opening drawers and peering under the bed. There was absolutely nothing to be seen. Whatever had been in the drawers was no longer there, and there weren't even any fluff balls under the bed. (I have masses of dog hairs under mine.)

Rather desperately we opened the wardrobe, but all we saw was a row of hangers without anything hanging on them. I felt goosebumps go thumping down my spine and wished we hadn't come. It was hard to believe that just a few weeks ago an old lady had been living there, all happily surrounded by her things. Her knick-knacks, as one of my grans calls them. Now it was like she had never been. No wonder Skye was so unhappy.

Mrs Solomons was waiting for us as we trailed back down the stairs.

"No luck? We've been through it with a fine tooth comb; it's hard to know where else to look. I'm afraid –" she patted Skye's shoulder – "you're going to have to reconcile yourself to the fact that we're not going to find it."

"We've *got* to find it," I said, as me and Jem went on our way. "You'd better have another talk to Saint Anthony."

"I can't do that," said Jem. "It would seem like nagging."

"You don't have to nag! Just apologise for bothering him and ask if he can get a bit of a move on. Only say it nicely, of course."

"He'll do it as fast as he can," said Jem. "You can't hurry a saint. He's probably busy."

I looked at her rather hard. "You did do what we agreed, didn't you? You did promise you'd go to church *every Sunday*?"

"I told him I'd go every Sunday that I could."

"That's not what we said!"

"You mean it's not what *you* said."

"But you agreed!"

"Excuse me," said Jem, "but who was talking to him, you or me? You don't know anything about these things! You wouldn't even know how to *begin* talking to someone like Saint Anthony. It's no use making promises you mightn't be able to keep."

I opened my mouth to protest, but Jem just went battering on without giving me a chance.

"Suppose I got the flu, or there was suddenly mountains of snow, or we got flooded, or something? That'd be an act of God. I could hardly be held responsible for an act of God!"

I still didn't see why she couldn't just have done what we agreed and promised to go every Sunday. Saint Anthony, presumably, being a saint, knew all about acts of God; he didn't need Jem reading him a lecture. Now he'd probably got the hump and wouldn't help us at all.

I said this to Jem and she went bright red and said, "That's blasphemy, that is!"

Now what was she on about?

"Taking his name in vain," said Jem. "You can't talk about a saint like that!"

"All I'm saying –" we'd reached Jem's block of flats, where we parted company – "I'm just *saying*, it would be nice if you could ask him to make Skye a priority. That's all."

I decided that I would give Saint Anthony until the weekend. If he hadn't made a move by then, it would have to be up to me. Which, as a matter of fact, it usually is. I've noticed this before. Skye does a lot of thinking, and Jem does a lot of talking, but I'm the one that takes action!

Jem was eager to know, next morning, whether anything had happened yet.

"Like… any clues, or anything?"

Skye said, "Why do you keep on about clues all the time?"

"I just wondered," said Jem.

"You heard what Mum said… I'll just have to accept that I'm never going to find Gran's pencil. Ever!"

"You might do," said Jem. "You shouldn't give up hope. I mean, look at my auntie."

I'm sure she thought she was being supportive, but I could see that all she was doing was making Skye even more upset than she already was. It would have made me upset if I'd had to hear about her auntie's engagement ring all over again. Well, what I mean, I *did* hear it all over again, but at least I hadn't just lost my gran.

I told Jem later that I didn't think she ought to keep asking Skye the same question over and over.

"She'll let us know if anything happens."

"But I did what you wanted!" said Jem. "I spoke to him again. Saint Anthony! I got back to him."

I think my mouth must have dropped open. I said, "*Really?*"

"Really! See, I thought about it, and I knew you couldn't do it, cos I mean you wouldn't know how, so I waited till I was in bed and then I had a word with him."

She made it sound incredibly important, *having a word with him*. But I guess it is pretty important, talking to a saint.

"What did you say?"

"I said –" Jem clasped her hands and tilted her face heavenwards – "I said, *Please, Saint Anthony, hear my prayer—*" She broke off at this point to explain that that was what you had to do. "Like, you can't just say 'Hi,' or 'Anybody there?' You have to use the right sort of language."

I said, "Yes, I can see that, but what exactly did you say?"

Jem tilted her face back up. *"Please, Saint Anthony, hear my prayer and help my friend Skye find her gran's pencil. And if you could be very kind and make it a priority, cos she's really, really miserable, I could probably manage to go to church every Sunday for at least a year."*

I said, *"Probably?* For a *year?"*

"I know," said Jem, "it's a terribly long time, but I thought it was the least I could do."

She was positively oozing with the spirit of self-sacrifice. I could almost see this little halo of light hovering just above her.

"I could hardly offer him anything less," said Jem. "Not if we want him to make it a priority."

I had actually been going to suggest she might have offered him more. I mean, what good was a year? Being a saint is pretty serious stuff, I would have thought. Saints *suffer.* Horrible things happen to them, like being pierced with

107

arrows and burned at the stake. I couldn't see Saint Anthony was going to be satisfied with one measly year. Seemed to me it was a bit of an insult, really.

I said this to Jem, but she rather pompously informed me that I had no idea what I was talking about. She said Saint Anthony hadn't been pierced with arrows *or* burned at the stake, and she reckoned a year was about right.

I said, "We shall see. I'm giving him till the weekend."

"Then what?" said Jem.

"Then I shall take over," I said.

Later that day, first period after lunch, we had PE. It was hockey with Miss Turnbull, and I just knew that everyone except me and Daisy Hooper were hoping it would rain. All the rest of my class are total wimps, like, "Yeeurgh, mud!" and "Ouch, my ankle!" and "Please, miss, can I be excused?" Skye says hockey is barbaric. Even Jem, who can run really fast when she wants, complains that it is pointless.

"Just churning up and down, whacking at things."

I happen to enjoy churning up and down. *And* whacking at things. So does Daisy. We are great rivals when it comes to hockey. Miss Turnbull always puts us on different teams and tells us to pick. Neither of us ever wants to pick Skye. Not even loyalty to a friend would make me pick her unless I absolutely had to cos of no one else being left.

Today she looked so forlorn, trailing her hockey stick behind her as if it were some kind of poisonous snake that might sink its fangs in her leg at any moment, that I went into total meltdown and heard myself calling her name before I properly realised what I was doing. Daisy shot me a look of triumph, like, "Gotcha!" Having Skye on your team means you are almost doomed to lose, and I do hate losing! Especially to Daisy. But I think it must be really humiliating to be left till last all the time, and Skye can't help being useless at sports. Jem simply can't be bothered, but Skye has no ball sense whatsoever, and I think her legs must be too long for her body, cos when she runs it's like she's wobbling about on stilts.

That day she was even more useless than usual. Miss Turnbull kept encouraging her to "Move, Skye! Move!" But then when she did move she got in people's way, and the game surged round her, with everyone yelling and sticks clashing, until in the end she just stopped dead, like she was confused by it all, and this huge great girl called Roseanne Stubbs charged into her and sent her flying. Miss Turnbull told her to go straight to the office and get herself checked out, and, oh yes, my team lost, which I'd known they would.

Skye didn't appear for our last class, and when we went to the office afterwards Mrs Tully said that she'd sent her home. I immediately texted her: *You OK?* She texted back, *Ha ha, got outa hockey!* Jem craned over to see.

"Oh, clever," she said. "She did it on purpose!"

But I didn't really think that she had.

"Just one more day," I said to Jem. "If nothing's happened by this time tomorrow…"

Jem said, "What?"

"I shall have to take matters into my own hands!"

The truth was, I was still feeling guilty in case it was my fault. *A treasured possession will be lost…* Suppose that really *was* the horoscope Skye had picked? Suppose I really *was* psychic?

"We can't afford to let things just dribble on."

"But you can't bully a saint," pleaded Jem. "Saint Anthony is very popular. He's one of the most popular saints there is. There's people all over the world asking him to find things for them. Surely we could just give him till Monday?"

I said grudgingly that I would think about it. I knew we couldn't expect an important saint like Saint Anthony to drop everything just for us. I could even see that some of the things people asked him to find might be considered more important than a mere pencil, even if it *was* a silver one and had belonged to Skye's beloved gran. A child, for instance, or a dog or a cat. They would probably be at the top of the list. Unless, of course, it was all done strictly in order, like first come, first served?

I asked Jem what she thought, but she crinkled her nose and admitted that she wasn't sure.

I said, "Well, I wish you'd find out. Couldn't you ask a priest or something?"

Jem said she didn't know any priests.

"You could always try going to church," I suggested. "Like you promised you would!"

She wriggled, uncomfortably. "I said if he helped us."

"Yes, but if you went *before* he helped us, that would show him you were serious."

I could tell she didn't want to. I had to remind her rather sternly that it was for Skye.

"It's not much to ask, I shouldn't have thought."

Jem agreed that it wasn't. She could hardly

do much else. I mean, just going to church! How difficult was that?

"So will you do it?"

She sighed. "I s'pose so."

"You promise?"

"Yes, all right!" she said. "I promise!"

So there I was, all prepared to give Saint Anthony another two days to get his act together, when this weird thing happened. Something very shocking. Mr Hargreaves handed back our maths homework and Skye had been given a B-. I could see it, in Mr Hargreaves's big, bullying handwriting, bursting off the page: B-. *Skye!* She'd never had such a low mark in her life before.

My first thought was that I was glad I hadn't done any copying off her. But then I caught sight of her face. All the colour had drained out of it so that she wasn't just ordinarily pale but white like a mushroom, with beads of sweat.

For a minute I was scared she might be going to faint. She used to faint sometimes at primary school when we had assemblies. I always thought it was something to do with her being so tall and the blood finding it difficult to get round her body, but I'd never known her to faint sitting down.

I was all prepared to spring into action when she took a deep breath, hooked her hair back over her ears and sat up very stiff and straight with this glassy smile on her lips. I wasn't sure whether Jem had noticed or not. I tried to catch her eye, but she was hunched over her maths book, drawing faces. She draws faces over everything. They all have these pouty lips and eyelashes sticking out like spokes. I poked at her, and nodded in Skye's direction. Jem craned over. She obviously saw the B−, cos she turned back to me, this look of total incredulity on her face.

As we filed out at the end of class Mr Hargreaves called Skye over to his desk. I heard him ask her, "What happened?" I could have told him. "Her gran has just died and she's very unhappy." Knowing Skye, though, she wouldn't say a word.

But that was it, as far as I was concerned. Saint Anthony had had his chance! I wasn't waiting any longer. I told Jem, who immediately said, "Does that mean I don't have to go to church on Sunday?"

"That is entirely up to you," I said. "We all have to do whatever we can."

"So what are you going to do?"

"I'm going to do what you suggested."

"Me?" Jem sounded surprised and pleased. "Did I suggest something?"

"You told me to go and look in my crystal ball," I said. "So that's what I'm going to do!"

CHAPTER SEVEN

One of my teachers once wrote on my school report that I was slapdash. Well, that is the way Mum interpreted it. What she actually said was, "Frankie must take care not to let her natural enthusiasm lead her astray."

Nothing whatsoever about being slapdash. It is true, however, I *suppose*, that I do sometimes get a bit carried away. It is difficult not to when you are eager to get on with things.

I was positively bursting to find Skye's pencil for

her, but I knew I couldn't just go rushing ahead. For a start, I had to find out about crystal balls and where you got them from. Could you simply go into a shop and buy one? If so, how much did they cost? Or maybe you could make them yourself. And then, once you'd made one, or at any rate got one, how did you use it?

I told Mum after tea that I was going upstairs to do my homework – without being told! She was well impressed. Once up there, I sat on the bed with my laptop to do research. They are always telling you at school that research is important.

"Don't just go straight to Wikipedia. Look around. Read as much as you can. Get a balanced view."

Well! It is all right *saying* this, and maybe it would work OK if we were all like Skye and could read at the rate of about a thousand words per minute, but when you are just an ordinary sort of person like the rest of us, it is not what I would call practical. I could have been there all night learning about crystal balls! Everybody said something different, and lots of the things they said I didn't properly understand, so that after a while I started to get a bit desperate. I'd boasted to Jem how I was going to use my powers, and I couldn't even work out how to begin!

I asked myself, what would Skye do? She wouldn't panic. She would… make a list! That was what she would do. Make a list of all the things you needed for a crystal ball, like:

1 A glass sphere

2 A crystal

3 Some incense

4 A silk scarf

I felt a bit better when I'd made my list. I could get all those things! No problem. A glass sphere was easy, I could use Mum's mixing bowl. A goldfish bowl would be better, but the secret of success, it seems to me, is making use of what you've got.

Like, for instance, I didn't have a crystal, but Angel

has a crystal necklace, which I reckoned would do just as well.

Like, again, we didn't have any incense, but we did have some stinky candles that someone gave Mum for Christmas. They were supposed to smell of sandalwood, but Dad said cow dung, more like, so Mum shut them away in a cupboard and forgot about them. She wouldn't mind if I used one.

The only scarves I have are thick and woolly, but Angel has this very expensive shawl that one of our grans brought back from holiday for her. It is all bright colours, like red and green and blue, very soft and slinky. Angel croons over it occasionally, and had it draped over her dressing table for a while, but she never actually wears it, so I didn't see she could object if I just borrowed it for a bit. It seemed to me it would be more suitable than one of my old woolly jobs. Apparently when you are doing a reading (that is, gazing into your crystal ball) it is very important to make an occasion of it. You can't just slap a mixing bowl on the kitchen table and drape a towel over your head, or the spirits will be insulted. I think this is perfectly understandable.

I was longing to get started, but I decided it would probably be best if I waited till next day, when Angel would be out of the house. She does get so ratty if anyone touches any of her things, and I knew if I asked her she'd only yell at me to keep my hands off. Plus she might let on to Mum, just to be mean, like, "Frankie's trying to tell fortunes with your mixing bowl!" Then Mum would get all fussed and bothered about me messing with the supernatural, and I couldn't do it anyway without Angel's shawl and her crystal necklace. I knew Mum would say I ought to ask first, but it wasn't like I was going to muck anything up. I was just going to *borrow* stuff, and put it straight back. Angel wouldn't ever need to find out. Even if she did, and went berserk, which she almost certainly would, it was a small price to pay for helping one of my best friends.

Next morning, Mum and Dad went off shopping.

Mum asked me if I'd like to go with them. She seemed somewhat surprised when I said I had things to do. She knows I adore shopping!

"Not more homework?" she said.

I told her that it was. Cos I mean it was; sort of. It certainly wasn't stuff that I could do at school. Dad said, "This is a turn-up for the books!" Meaning, I *think*, that it was somewhat unusual, not to say practically unheard of, for me to choose homework over shopping, but Mum told him not to tease.

"We should be encouraging her. Good for you, Frankie! Angel, do you want a lift into town?"

I held my breath. It would be just like Angel to have fallen out with all her friends and to stay sulking on her own indoors. I'm surprised she ever has any friends since she is so bad-tempered, though strangely enough there are some people who actually seem to like her. Maybe she doesn't yell at them the way she does at me.

Anyway, to my relief, she came skittering downstairs screeching at the top of her voice that she was coming, she was coming. "Don't go without me!" She was all dressed up in bright purple leggings and knee-length boots with heels about two metres high, which was why she was skittering. She looked like the leaning tower of Pisa in a high wind.

A few minutes later I heard the car doors slam and the engine start up. Hooray! I had the place to myself. Well, apart from Tom, but he doesn't count. He was up in his room playing on the computer, and even if he came down he wouldn't be interested in what I was doing. He might give one of his grunts, like "Hm?" to acknowledge my presence; but then again, if his head was filled with computer stuff, he mightn't even do that. I don't think he really notices other people.

Determined to be businesslike, I consulted my list: sphere – crystal – incense – scarf. First off, I cleaned the kitchen table. Then I took down Mum's big glass mixing bowl and washed it and dried it and polished it till it sparkled. I didn't want to give the spirits any excuse to feel I wasn't treating them with proper respect.

Next I tiptoed up the stairs and into Angel's room for her crystal necklace and her shawl. I was careful to make a note not only of which drawer she kept the shawl in, but whereabouts in the drawer she kept it, so that I could put it back in exactly the right place. Like the necklace. *Under* the bracelet with the red stones, on *top* of the butterfly hair slide. She'd know immediately if anything was even just a centimetre away from where it ought to be. She is totally obsessive.

Lastly, I rooted about in the kitchen cupboard in search of a stinky candle. Got it!

I put the necklace in the bowl, lit the candle, draped my head in the shawl and settled down to wait. Rags settled down with me, his front legs sprawled across a chair, his eyes firmly fixed on me and the mixing bowl.

We waited and waited, but nothing seemed to be happening. Surely something ought to happen?

I'd thought a mist was meant to form. Then when you asked your question, shapes would appear and you had to interpret them. Like, maybe, what I was hoping, I'd see the shape of a piece of furniture, or Skye's garden, and I'd know that was where the pencil was to be found. Only there wasn't any mist, there weren't any shapes, there wasn't anything!

Rags gave an impatient yelp. He is always very interested in what is going on, but he does expect a bit of action. So do I!

I was just beginning to despair when I had this bright idea, thus showing that I do sometimes pay attention in science classes whatever Mrs Monteith might say to the contrary. If I put some boiling water in the mixing bowl and covered the bowl with the shawl, the water would condense and form a mist. Yay! There is always a solution to every problem if you just come at it the right way.

I boiled the kettle and very carefully poured the water up to the halfway mark. Then I put the candle in as well, standing it on an upturned dish. I reckoned the candle would keep the water heated up and help the mists to form, as well as creating a suitable atmosphere. I felt the spirits would appreciate a bit of sandalwood. I mean, it is quite an exotic sort of scent. I am not sure where it comes from. India, maybe. Somewhere mysterious, at any rate.

I slid back under the shawl and made a tent over the bowl. It was rather hot under there, what with the candle and the boiling water, and the smell was a bit overpowering, but sometimes, in a good cause, you have to be prepared to suffer. I wondered if there was some special spirit language you were supposed to use, or whether you could ask questions in ordinary English, except that ordinary English was all I knew so I didn't really have much choice. I began to chant, very low:

"Where is the pencil, I'm looking for the pencil… spirits, speak! Where is the pencil?"

Rags woofed hopefully. At last! Something was happening!

I wasn't actually sure that it was, but I kept on with my chanting.

"Where is the pencil… spirits, speak!"

Suddenly, from somewhere behind me, came a ghostly wail: "Whooooo aaaaaah! The spirits speak!"

I sprang round, sending the mixing bowl crashing to the floor.

"*Tom!* You *idiot!*"

I screamed it at him. He stood there, grinning.

"What's going on?"

"Nothing's going on!" Since when did Tom take any interest in other people's activities? "I'm unblocking my sinuses, if you must know."

It's what Dad does when he gets stuffed up. He says his sinuses are blocked and he has to inhale over hot water.

Tom seemed to find it funny. He said, "So what's all this about spirits?"

I glared at him. "Didn't anyone ever tell you it's rude to eavesdrop?"

"I wasn't eavesdropping! *I* didn't know you were down here. Is that Angel's shawl you're wearing?"

"I'm putting it straight back," I said. "I haven't done anything to it!"

"Just touching it'd be enough," said Tom.

"Not if she doesn't know."

"She'll find out. She always does. Then you'll be for it!"

"So don't tell her!"

"Won't have to. She'll just know. *And* you've broken Mum's bowl."

I turned to look at it.

"*And* the floor's all wet."

"Well, and whose fault is that?" I said crossly. "Coming down here making spooky noises! What are you doing down here, anyway? I thought you were upstairs?"

"I was," said Tom. "Now I've come down here. I suppose I can move about if I want?"

Well, he could, but it wasn't what he normally

did. He normally stayed in his room for hours on end. Why *today*?

"You'd better mop that floor," he said. "You know what happened last time… Mum nearly broke her neck."

He helped himself to something out of the fridge and went off, eating. Rags gazed wistfully after him, his nostrils twitching. Food is *such* a big thing in the life of a dog! But he is very loyal. He settled down to watch as I crawled about on my hands and knees, picking up bits of mixing bowl. Mum was not going to be pleased, but at least I could make sure the floor was nice and dry, so she wouldn't be able to complain about *that*.

I folded Angel's shawl and wiped her crystal necklace on a sheet of kitchen roll, then took them back upstairs to her room. I put them away *exactly* as I had found them. No way could she ever suspect I had been there.

On my way back along the landing I heard the sound of a car pulling into the drive and knew that Mum and Dad had returned. Rags gave one of his loud, happy barks and went galloping off to greet them, nearly throwing me over as he did so. Angel complains that he's an ill-mannered yob, but he's like me, he gets enthusiastic. Not that I was feeling very enthusiastic right at that moment. I was actually tempted to turn round and go hide in my bedroom, but I knew it would only be putting off the evil moment. Mum was bound to discover sooner or later.

Oops! She already had... She was looking in the pedal bin even as I breezed my way through the kitchen door. I was still hoping that maybe she wouldn't yet have found out, which was why I chose to breeze rather than slink. If you slink, it makes you look guilty. But breezing didn't deceive Mum for one second.

"Frankie?" she said. "What happened with my mixing bowl?"

Immediately assuming I was the one to blame. Not Tom; not Angel. *Me.*

"I'm waiting," said Mum.

"I'm really sorry," I said, "it was an accident."

"Well, I didn't imagine you'd done it on purpose! I was just wondering," said Mum, "what you were doing with it at all? I thought you were supposed to be getting on with your homework?"

For a minute I had this wild idea of claiming that it *was* homework, like making something for technology. Trouble was, I couldn't think what I might be making. Last week we'd done soup, but you don't need a mixing bowl for that.

"Still waiting," said Mum.

I had to tell her *something*. "I was unblocking my sinuses," I said. "Like Dad."

"Dad doesn't go smashing my mixing bowls, and what's wrong with your sinuses, anyway?"

I sniffed. "They're blocked. I'm all stuffed up."

"Rubbish!" said Mum.

"I could have a polyp," I said. A girl at school had had a polyp. It used to plop in and out of her nose and make you feel sick. She had it removed in the end.

"I don't see any signs of a polyp," said Mum. "I hope you're not turning into a hypochondriac."

Whatever that is.

"Someone who imagines they've got things wrong with them when they haven't," said Mum. "The only thing wrong with you, my girl, is that you don't seem to have any sort of control over your movements!"

I felt like pointing out that that in itself could be a symptom of some kind of fatal disease, and that any normal mother would take it seriously, but I thought perhaps I'd better not.

"I wiped the floor for you," I said. "It's dry as can be!"

She didn't even praise me for making such a good job of it. I really do wonder, sometimes, if it's worth bothering.

Jem called me later, wanting to know how I'd got on.

"Did you discover anything?"

I told her no, Tom had come barging in making stupid noises and upset me.

"It's a very delicate operation," I said. "You need absolute peace and quiet."

"So are you going to try again?"

I'd thought about that, but the only other mixing bowl Mum had was a tiny one. Plus I didn't fancy my chances a second time, creeping into Angel's room and helping myself to her things.

"I reckon I'm going to try something else," I said.

"What? What are you going to try?"

"I'm going to try a pendulum."

It was something I'd read on the Internet, when I was researching about crystal balls.

"A pendulum like on a necklace?" said Jem.

"That's a *pendant*," I said. "Pendulum's what you get on a clock. Thing that swings to and fro."

"Oh."

There was a silence.

"It's dead easy," I said. "Anybody can make one. Though not everybody, of course, has the power to make them work." I added this just in case she was getting any ideas in her head. "You have to be a bit psychic. I'll probably try it out tonight, see what answers I get."

Making a pendulum was ever so much simpler than making a crystal ball. All you needed was a key, preferably an ancient one, and a piece of cord eighteen centimetres long. What you did, you attached the key to one end of the cord, then held the other end so that the key could dangle to and fro. Easy peasy! If you were psychic. It wasn't any use Jem thinking she could do it.

The oldest key I could find was the tiny little one belonging to the corner cabinet that stands in my bedroom and used to belong to one of my grans. I reckoned that would be plenty old enough. I didn't have any cord, and didn't quite like to go and root about among Mum's sewing stuff, but there was a ball of string in one of the kitchen drawers, so I carefully measured off eighteen centimetres on my ruler and went upstairs to shut myself away where I wouldn't be disturbed.

Now all I had to do was ask questions, but they had to be questions that could be answered with a simple yes or no. If the key swung in a north to south direction, it was giving the answer *yes*. If it swung east to west, that meant *no*. And if it went round in circles it was probably better for you not to know. I did hope it didn't go in circles!

I only had one small problem: I had no idea which was north and which was south! I bucketed downstairs to ask Dad. He was watching football on television and pointed silently towards the windows. Right! Now I could get going.

I held my end of the cord and waited till the key had settled down. OK! I took a breath.

"Do you know where Skye's silver pencil is?"

Yikes! It did! North to south: that meant *yes*. This was very encouraging! I asked another question.

"Is it in Skye's back garden?"

To my disappointment, the key immediately set off in a circle. *Better not to know.* But why?

I tried again.

"Should we look in Skye's back garden?"

This time, the key swung north to south. That was better! But I had to be sure.

"Is that where the pencil is? In the back garden?"

East to west: *no.* This wasn't making any sense! What was the point of looking in the garden if the pencil wasn't there?

"Please concentrate," I said. "*Is the pencil in Skye's back garden?*"

Yes.

"So is that where we should look?"

No.

Excuse me???

"You just said that that's where it was!"

The key looped about, irritably. I waited for it to calm down.

"Sorry," I said. "Sorry! I just wanted to make sure… *is the pencil in the back garden?*"

I waited. The key hung sullenly. I'd obviously upset it.

"Or is it somewhere else?"

No response.

"Please," I begged, *"speak to me!"*

Still nothing. Bother. Bother, bother, *bother*! I tossed the key across the room. I knew there wasn't any point in carrying on. Spirits are extremely sensitive and can also be rather prickly. I had read this somewhere. It is essential to treat them with respect. Once they are displeased with you they won't communicate no matter how hard you try. You can plead as much as you like.

I would have to find another way. A new set of spirits. And this time I would take care not to say anything that might cause offence.

I was still trying to think what I might do when my phone rang and it was Jem, calling to inform me – what utter cheek! – that she had just tried "the pendulum thing" for herself. I was distinctly annoyed. What right had she to go trying it? I was the one that had discovered it; I was the one that was psychic. Probably. Maybe. Jem certainly wasn't!

She told me that it was all a load of rubbish. "I asked it if it knew where the pencil was and it said at the North Pole!"

I was glad it hadn't worked for her any more than it had worked for me, but the *North Pole*?

"Dunno how that happened," I said. "You're only s'posed to ask it things it can answer yes or no to."

"I know *that*," said Jem. "I read all about it."

"So how come it said the North Pole?"

"Cos I asked it! I got sick of it just swinging about, not making any sense, so I said, 'Is it at the North Pole?' Like testing it, you know? See if it knew what it was doing. And it obviously didn't, cos it said yes. Which, I mean, is just stupid!"

I said, "Like I told you, you have to be psychic."

"You think you are?" said Jem.

Omigod, she was so jealous!

"I must be a bit," I said.

"Why? Did yours work?"

"Sort of."

"What's that mean?"

"I asked if it knew where the pencil was and it said yes, but it refused to tell me where."

Jem said, "Huh!"

"It's my fault, I upset it. I got impatient."

"Like you did with Saint Anthony, keeping on nagging at him."

"*I* didn't nag him! I told you to ask him nicely and promise you'd go to church every Sunday and you didn't, you were *grudging*. I'm not surprised he didn't help us!"

"He still could," said Jem.

I said, "Yeah, and pigs could fly!"

We didn't exactly quarrel, but we both rang off in something of a huff. I thought it was really sad that Jem should be so envious of my psychic powers that she resented my little bit of success. I had, after all, proved that the spirits knew where the pencil was. It was just a question of getting them to tell me.

Oh, and I nearly forgot. Later that evening Angel came roaring downstairs like one demented, wanting to know if I had been in her room.

I said, "*Me?*"

She screamed, "Who else?"

She really is quite unbalanced. I asked her what made her think anyone in their right mind would *want* to go in her room, at which she turned bright purple and screeched, "Did you or didn't you?"

Fortunately at that point Mum stepped in to say that *she* had gone in to check the central heating, which calmed the mad woman down a bit, though she still regarded me with suspicion. Mum seemed to think it was funny.

"Are you checking up on us?" she said.

Darkly, Angel muttered that she'd found a bit of mud on one of her rugs. "Like someone had come in from the garden."

Oops! That would have been me. I'd been out

there, playing with Rags. Tom mouthed at me across the room: "Told you so!"

It was a nasty moment.

CHAPTER EIGHT

Although I say it myself, I am not the sort of person that is easily put off. Some people, when there are setbacks, will say, "Oh, I have had enough of this, I cannot be bothered," but with me it is just the opposite. With me it is more like, *No way am I going to give up!* I don't mean to boast; it is just how I am. I cannot rest until I have done what I set out to do, which in this case was find Skye's pencil for her. There had to be other ways of using my psychic ability!

Sunday morning, I found Angel in the bathroom doing things with her hair. She is always doing things with her hair.

"What do you want?" she said.

I told her I didn't want anything. "I just happened to be passing."

"Well, I just happen to be in here!"

And Mum just happened to be downstairs in the kitchen. I seized the opportunity.

"I s'pose you don't happen to know what it's called when people sit around a table and conjure up spirits?"

I was proud of that phrase, *conjure up spirits*. I wasn't totally absolutely certain what it meant, but I knew it was the right one to use. Angel gave this sharp bark of laughter.

"You mean spirits like whisky and gin, and they all get drunk?"

Honestly, Angel has even less sense of humour than Skye. That is why it is so pathetic when she tries making a joke. It is simply not funny.

I said, "No. When they sit in the dark and hold hands and someone goes into a trance and a spirit comes down and they ask it questions and it gives them the answers."

Angel said, "Oh, you mean *that* sort of spirit. I thought you meant the sort Dad likes to drink at Christmas!"

Ha ha ha. I almost began to wish I'd never asked her. She is *such* hard work.

"So what's it called?" I said. "It's called something!"

Angel threw her hair back over her shoulders, splattering me with water.

"Seance?" she said.

Say-onss. "How d'you spell it?"

"S.e.a.n.c.e. Don't they teach you people *anything*?"

I said, "Mostly just useless stuff. What's that other one, where you all put your fingers on a glass and the glass moves round the table spelling things out?"

"How should I know?" said Angel. And then

rather grudgingly, "I suppose you're talking about a Ouija board?"

"Yes!" I pounced eagerly. I'd heard of Ouija boards. "How d'you spell that one?"

"I haven't the faintest idea! Why ask me? Go and look it up."

I said, "How can I do that if I don't know how to spell it?"

"Use your brain for once! If you've got one. I don't see why you should keep picking mine all the time. Why are you asking about all this weird stuff?"

"It's for homework," I said.

She probably didn't believe me, but so what? Wasn't any business of hers, anyway.

I went back to my room and opened up my laptop to find out about seances and Ouija boards. Seance was easy. There's oceans and oceans about seances. I wrote down all that I needed to know, then tried "Weeja". I didn't think anything would come up, but computers can be really clever at times, guessing what you want even when you can't spell it right. Other times I find they can be completely maddening, like if you run two words together by mistake and they say they don't know what you're talking about. I mean, that is just *stupid*. But I put in "Weeja" and it came right back at me: *Ouija*. That is so neat!

I didn't bother taking any more notes cos a) I was tired of writing things down and b) I really actually did have homework to do. In any case, I was hoping if we had a seance, I would find a spirit that was willing to help.

The biggest difficulty, I thought, would be convincing Skye. I reckoned she'd say it was all rubbish and a waste of time, but when I put it to her next morning on the way to school, she didn't raise any objections. She wasn't exactly what I'd call eager, but she agreed we might as well give it a go.

"I s'pose it can't hurt."

"Might be fun," urged Jem. "When shall we do it?"

I'd have liked to get going that same day, but I felt we really needed a whole evening.

"We shouldn't rush things. Not if we want the spirits to speak to us."

"So when, then?"

We decided that Friday after school Jem and Skye would come back with me for a sleepover.

"That way we can wait till it's properly dark."

Jem said, "Yes, cos that's when the spirits are most likely to come."

"You know it's all rubbish," said Skye.

But I had this feeling she was only saying it cos she felt she had to. She wanted so much to find her gran's pencil that she was willing to try anything. I said later to Jem, "I do hope it works! But even if it doesn't, I'm not going to give up."

My bedroom is about the size of a broom cupboard, so when Jem and Skye stay over, it is a bit of a crush, but we don't mind. Skye always brings her sleeping bag, while Jem and me cram together in my bed.

Rags usually crams with us, flolloping about on top of the duvet and making Jem squeal when she wakes up in the middle of the night to find his big furry head right next to her on the pillow.

So, on Friday evening, we all rushed upstairs as soon as we'd finished tea. It wasn't yet properly dark, not inky black dark, but as I said, we had to prepare. I'd made a list of all the stuff we'd need. I was getting quite good at lists!

"Number one," I said, "a table and chairs."

Skye gazed round. "Where d'you think we're going to put them?"

I had to admit that was a bit of a problem.

"Maybe we should have done it at my place?"

I said, "No, it's got to be here." It was just this feeling I had. Skye's bedroom might be bigger, but it is not what I would call spirit-friendly. It is too clean and tidy. "I'll ask Mum if we can bring her little table up from the front room. That'll fit in. Then we can all sit round it on the floor. OK! Number two: food."

"*Food?* How long are we going to be here?"

"It's not for us," I said. "It's for the spirits."

Somewhat surprised, Jem said, "Do spirits get hungry?"

I wasn't sure about this. I just knew that that's what it had said. You had to put something out for them, like a bowl of soup or a slice of bread.

"Maybe it depends how long they've been dead," said Jem. "Prob'ly takes a while before they realise they don't have to keep eating all the time."

I glanced rather anxiously at Skye. Trust Jem to go talking about dead people!

"I think it's more just good manners," I said. "Like when someone calls round you offer them a cup of tea? So you offer the spirits a bit of bread."

"But how can they eat?" said Jem. "If they're spirits? They don't have any mouths!"

"Does it really matter?" said Skye. She sounded like she was growing restive, like she was impatient to get started. "What else do we need?"

I consulted my list. "Three candles."

"Why three?" said Jem.

"*I* don't know! Cos that's what it said."

"Why couldn't we just have the light on?"

"Cos they prefer candles! We have to make them feel welcome. 'Sides, candles are warm. It's prob'ly cold where they are."

"What, out in space?"

"Out there." I waved a hand. "Drifting about. They see a bit of candlelight, they're going to think, *Oh, these people have made an effort, I'll go down and find out what they want.*"

Jem said, "Mm." She seemed suddenly doubtful. "Do we *really* expect them to come?"

"Not much point doing it if we don't," said Skye. "I mean, it's all a load of rubbish, but – well!" She gave a little laugh, like she'd embarrassed herself. "We don't necessarily understand everything that goes on."

"This is it," I said. "Life is full of mysteries. Let's go and get all the stuff!"

I asked Mum if we could borrow her small table, and she not only said yes, but actually got Tom to carry it upstairs for us. I didn't ask if I could have some of her candles cos I reckoned she'd only get in a flap and think we were going to burn the house down, so I secretly helped myself to three of the little stinky ones from the kitchen cupboard. I also took a slice of bread out of the bread bin. I'd have liked to put some peanut butter on it, cos I mean dry bread is hardly very enticing, but just as I was about to open the fridge, Angel came in.

She screeched, "Omigod, you're eating again!" in tones of complete hysteria. "You've only just had tea!"

I didn't feel inclined to get into conversation with Angel right at that moment, plus Jem was standing there in full view, clutching candles, so I said grandly that the bread wasn't for me, it was for the birds, and I was going to scatter it out of my bedroom window. As we scuttled back upstairs Jem hissed, "Bread is bad for birds!"

I said, "Yes, I know. You're supposed to give them seeds."

"So why are you—" She stopped. "Oh! That was just an excuse for Angel."

I looked at her. Rather hard.

"I can't help it," whined Jem. "I'm tired! I've been up all day."

"Maybe," I said kindly, "you should go to bed and we'll wake you up when we're ready to start. After all, it's nearly seven o'clock… *way* past your little kiddy bedtime!"

"I didn't hardly sleep last night," said Jem. "I kept having these nightmares."

"How d'you have nightmares when you're not asleep?"

"I said I didn't *hardly* sleep. I kept being woken up. It's scary," said Jem, "messing with dead people."

"We're not messing with them," I said. "We're just inviting them – *politely* – to come and talk to us. They don't have to if they don't want to."

"But what happens –" Jem lowered her voice to a whisper as we approached the bedroom, where we had left Skye – "what happens if one of them is

Skye's gran?"

"That's what we're hoping for," I said. "That's what we *want*. Then we can ask her questions about the pencil, like 'Do you remember where you put it?' kind of thing. There wouldn't be anything scary about it!"

Jem seemed unconvinced. I did hope she wasn't going to develop cold feet at the last moment.

Skye and I agreed that although by now it was quite dark we ought to wait until it was really *dark* dark, so for a couple of hours we listened to music and played games on the computer. By nine o'clock we couldn't wait any longer.

"If we're going to do it, let's do it!" said Skye.

Suddenly, she was really keen. Jem was the one who was dithering. She said she'd been thinking about things and she wasn't sure it was right to try and speak to dead people, she wasn't sure the Church would approve.

I said, "Church? What church? You never go to church!" Which pretty well killed *that* argument.

So then she starts wittering about evil spirits. How did we know evil spirits weren't going to come swarming down? I couldn't immediately think of an answer to that one. It was Skye, in her best no-nonsense voice, who briskly informed Jem there were no such things as evil spirits, it was just superstition.

"It's all rubbish, anyway."

"So why are we doing it?" wailed Jem.

"Cos it wouldn't be fair on Frankie if we didn't. She's gone to a lot of trouble setting it all up."

"Just wants to prove she's psychic," muttered Jem.

I ignored this. "I'm going downstairs," I said, "to tell Mum we don't want to be disturbed. You get the candles lit – and don't let Rags eat the bread!" He'd been greedily eyeing it for some time. Dad says he's like a walking dustbin.

"He shouldn't really be in here," said Skye. "Not if we're having a proper seance."

What did she know? She thought it was all

rubbish, anyway.

"He'll be OK," I said. "Spirits like animals."

I wasn't turning the poor boy out! It was his bedroom as much as mine.

I couldn't find Mum or Dad. I found Tom instead, watching some dreary documentary sort of thing on the television. I said, "Where's Mum and Dad?"

Tom said, "Gone to a meeting."

"When are they coming back?"

"Dunno. Didn't say. 'Bout 'leven o'clock? I've been left here to look after you," said Tom.

"Well, just to let you know," I said, "we're rehearsing something *very important* for school and we don't want to be disturbed. OK?"

He raised a hand. "'Kay."

Jubilantly, I hammered back upstairs.

"Mum and Dad have gone out! There's only Tom."

Not even Angel. We were safe!

I switched off the light and we all sat cross-legged on the floor, holding hands, round Mum's little low table. It was cosy in the flickering glow of the candles.

"OK! So what do we do?" said Skye.

I said, to begin with we all had to chant.

"Like what? What do we chant?"

I put on my chanting voice that I'd been practising. "*Alakazam, alakazoo…*"

"Which means what?"

"Doesn't mean anything. They're just magic words, like *abracadabra*. It's what's called *creating an atmosphere*. You have to have an atmosphere. Soon as it seems right, I'll call on the spirits. What I'll do, I'll ask if there's anyone there, and if there is they'll rap, like this –" I tapped my fingers on the table – "or make some sort of noise, so that we'll know. Then we can start asking questions, like 'Are you Skye's gran?' and 'Are you happy?' and 'Can you tell us where your pencil is?' sort of thing."

"S'pose it's not Skye's gran?"

"Well, then I'll ask if they can find her for us. They're bound to all know each other. I'd say, 'Have you met a lady called Mrs Samuels who arrived just recently?'" I felt Skye's hand quiver in mine. "If your gran's there," I said, "I bet she'd be really pleased to know you're thinking about her."

Skye didn't say anything, just nodded.

"It's not going to upset you, is it?" said Jem. "I don't think we ought to do it if it's going to upset you!"

"Just get on with it," muttered Skye.

I began my chant: "*Alakazam, alakazoo…*"

The others joined in. We all swayed slightly to the rhythm.

"*Alakazam, alakazoo…*"

It was all going fine until Jem had to cry out and break the spell.

"I don't like this!" she wailed. "It's spooky!"

Skye told her somewhat sharply to be quiet. I was more than a little annoyed with her myself. I'd been starting to have these excited tinglings all up and down my spine, which made me think there must be spirits somewhere close by. Now Jem had probably gone and frightened them off.

"Start again," said Skye. "And, you!" She thumped Jem's hand on the table. "Don't interrupt!"

We resumed our chanting. *"Alakazam, alakazoo…"*

The tingles went trickling again down my spine. It felt like little ghost fingers tapping on my bones. I definitely had this feeling that we were not alone. Something was out there!

A wave of psychic power washed over me.

"Spirits, speak! We're looking for Skye's gran. Her name is Mrs Samuels. She's out there somewhere. Please, if you know her, ask her to come down!"

There was a silence. And then I heard it… a faint whiffle, like the breathing of a ghostly creature. Skye's fingers dug hard into mine. Jem made a little choking sound.

"Spirits," I cried, "answer!"

We held our breath. The whiffling came again, followed by a long, mournful moaning. Jem screeched and tore her hand out of mine. I felt Skye tremble.

She pointed, with quivering finger. I turned to look. A dark and hideous shape was slowly rising out of the gloom.

Jem screeched again. She sprang to her feet and tore across the room, screaming as she went. We heard her feet thudding down the stairs. Me and Skye clung to each other, paralysed with fear as the shape came towards us.

"What is it?" whispered Skye.

CHAPTER NINE

We watched in frozen horror as the dark shape moved towards us. Suddenly, with a bound, it was on the table. Skye gave a terrified "Eek!" and fell backwards. I tried to scream, but nothing happened. And then I felt it. Something rough and prickly brushing against me. With a strangulated yelp, I tore across the room and switched on the light.

"*Rags!*"

He stood there on the table, sheepishly wagging, the slice of bread clamped between his jaws. I hadn't the heart to take it off him. I was just so relieved he wasn't an evil spirit!

Skye, rather crossly, picked herself up. "I told you he shouldn't be in here!"

To be honest, I'd forgotten all about him. He had obviously been curled up under the duvet. He would probably have stayed there quite happily if it hadn't been for the lure of the bread. I said this to Skye, but she just harrumphed and said again that she had told me so.

"He should have been shut out. You can't have a proper seance with a dog in the room! Not one like him, anyway."

We both looked across at Rags, chomping on his bread.

"We can always get some more," I said.

"Yes, and next time maybe you'll listen to me!"

I do so hate it when people keep on. I mean, what is the point? It's hardly very helpful.

"We'd better go and find Jem," I said, "before she screams the place down."

Jem was in the sitting room with Tom and – omigod! *Angel.* Jem was burbling and flapping her arms about.

"What's going on?" said Angel. "What have you been up to?"

"Nothing," I said. It is my standard reply. Whenever Angel wants to know what I've been up to, I always say "Nothing". Sometimes I get away with it; sometimes I don't. I knew today I wouldn't. Not with Jem gibbering and carrying on.

"So why is she in this state?" said Angel. Her eyes narrowed. "I hope you haven't been doing anything stupid? I'm responsible for you when Mum and Dad are out!"

Really? First I'd heard of it.

"I thought he was," I said, pointing at Tom.

"Only if I'm not here."

"Which you weren't," I said.

"Well, I am now."

Unfortunately.

"Look! *You.*" Angel poked a finger at Jem. "Just

stop thrashing around!" Angel was starting to sound exasperated. Jem can get to you like that. "I demand to know what you've been up to!"

"It's all right." Skye stepped in, very calm and collected. "We thought we saw a ghost, that's all."

"Dude!" Tom sprang up, excited. "What sort of ghost? Headless?"

Quickly, before Jem could start wailing, I said, "It wasn't a ghost, it was Rags. He was under the duvet and we didn't know he was there."

"He rose up," said Skye, "in the darkness."

Angel pounced. "What darkness?" Her nostrils flared, like she sensed she was on to something. "You've been doing things!" she said. "All that weird stuff you were asking about… you've been doing it!"

Tom cried, "Whoa!"

"You be quiet," snapped Angel. "You were supposed to be keeping an eye on them!"

"He was," I said, "until you came in."

"Just as well I did come in. People practising black

magic all over the place!"

Jem gave a howl.

"Now see what you've done!" screamed Angel.

I said, "*Me?* I haven't done anything!"

"You've gone and set her off again!"

"That was *you*," I said, "going on about black magic. I don't know why you're making all this fuss. All it was, was just an ordinary little seance, same as anybody might have. Nothing *black* about it! We just wanted to talk to S—"

"Oh, SHUT UP!" roared Angel. "Wittering on! Can't you see she's in shock?"

We all turned to stare at Jem. She'd quietened down for a few seconds, but on hearing that she was in shock, she immediately started up again.

"This is cool," said Tom.

I thought for a minute that Angel was going to have some kind of fit. Like her head was going to burst open and her brains come spilling out.

"Just stop it, stop it!" she shouted. "Stop

making all this noise! *You.*" She gave me a shove. "Get her into the kitchen!"

"What for?"

"Just do it!" bawled Angel. She was making more noise than anyone, but it seemed unwise to cross her. Between us, me and Skye hauled Jem to her feet.

"What's in the kitchen?" said Skye.

"Tea," said Angel.

Jem gave a smothered shriek.

"She doesn't drink tea," I said. "She doesn't like it."

"You'd rather she died of shock?"

Jem stared, her eyes like satellite dishes. "I'm going to *die*?"

Honestly! She is such a drama queen.

I said, "This is stupid! It was only *Rags.*"

"Rising up," said Tom, "in the darkness… *whoo hah*!" He waggled his hands above his head. Jem gave a short sharp scream.

"Will everybody just stop PANICKING!" roared Angel. "Get her out there!"

We practically had to drag Jem through to the kitchen. She was now convinced that her last hour had come, and Tom didn't help, making his stupid hooting noises. We watched as Angel viciously smashed a tea bag in a mug of boiling water and dumped about half a kilo of sugar on top of it.

"There!" She thrust the mug at Jem, who shrank back piteously, moaning that sugar wasn't good for you.

"Just drink it!" snarled Angel. "I'm not going to be held responsible for you collapsing."

I was sort of impressed in spite of myself. I mean, it was totally ridiculous, but who would have thought Angel could be so ruthlessly efficient in a crisis? Not that it *was* a crisis, except in her own mind, and now, probably, in Jem's. Left to ourselves, me and Skye would have snapped Jem out of it in no time. Angel claimed later that she had "risen to the occasion".

"Just as well *one* of us managed to keep her head."

We all watched with interest as Jem, blubbering to herself, noisily slurped down the tea. I wondered if she would be sick. That is her normal trick when forced to swallow something she doesn't want. She used to throw up regularly at primary school, but Angel had obviously scared her, cos the tea stayed down.

"I don't want to die!" she whimpered.

I said, "You weren't ever going to die. Nothing happened!"

"Will you *please* keep quiet?" said Angel. "I'm doing my best to administer a bit of first aid!"

"So now you've administered it," I said, "we could go back upstairs."

Angel seemed reluctant to let us leave. It was like she'd got herself into a position of power and was determined to hang on to it as long as possible.

"It'd probably be safer if you stayed down here for a bit."

"We don't want to stay down here!" Apart from anything else, Mum and Dad could come back at any minute. I had this feeling Mum might not be too pleased if she discovered about the seance. But then she might not be too pleased with Angel, either. After all, she was the one that had told me about seances. I hadn't even known what they were called until I asked her.

Cunningly, I said, "When are Mum and Dad due back?"

I saw Angel's eyes flicker towards the kitchen clock.

"We'd have to tell them what happened," I said. "Then Mum would want to know how I'd found out about seances and I'd have to say that you told me."

Angel was indignant. "I did no such thing!"

"You told me how to spell it."

"So what? I didn't tell you to go and do it!"

"You should have checked," I said. "We're only young, we're not responsible."

Angel's face turned a sort of mottled beetroot.

"You are an utterly repulsive child," she said. "I don't wish to have anything more to do with you!"

I said, "Good. So we can go back upstairs."

"Go and see if there are any more ghosts," said Tom. "*Whoo-aaah!*"

He is not usually that silly. As a rule it is difficult to get him to say anything at all.

"Have you been at Dad's whisky?" I said.

Tom looked hurt. "I don't touch whisky, I'm a teetotaller!"

Jem giggled, in a slightly mad fashion.

"She's gone and overdosed on sugar," said Tom.

We managed at last to get back upstairs. It wasn't till we were safely in my bedroom that Skye, with an air of guilty triumph, slid her hand up her sweater and produced a slice of bread.

"I took it from the bread bin," she said. She smiled, hopefully. "I thought we could… you know! Try again?"

If it had been up to me I'd have said no problem. Go for it! But that is just me. I suppose I am a bit bold. Plus I felt really sorry for Skye. In spite of reckoning it was all rubbish, she was obviously desperate to have another go. But Jem was already starting to look apprehensive.

"We're not doing it *again*?"

Skye's face fell. "I thought you wanted to help me find Gran's pencil?"

"I do," said Jem, "I do! But I don't want to do a seance again!"

"Don't worry," I said. "I've got loads of ideas. I'll think of something!"

Over the weekend, Angel kept glowering at me and Tom kept flapping his hands and going "*Whoo haah!*" in this silly, high flutey voice. Mum looked at him in surprise.

"I think he's going senile," I said. "Either that or he's been at the whisky."

Mum said, "Tom?"

"I told you," said Tom, "I'm a teetotaller."

"So what's with all the whooing and hahing?" said Mum.

Tom sent me this sly glance. "We reckon there's

a ghost in the house."

"Rubbish," said Mum. "Total nonsense!"

I was glad that Mum was so sensible and down to earth. It would have been awkward if she'd asked questions. I really thought I'd got away with it.

But then, on Monday morning…

"I've been having nightmares," said Jem. "All weekend!"

She announced it proudly, like it was some sort of special accomplishment. Like she'd won a competition or got an A for her maths homework.

"I woke up *screaming*," she said. "Mum came rushing in thinking I was being murdered!"

"But nothing happened," I said. "Why are you having nightmares all about nothing?"

"It was scary," said Jem. She tossed her head, defiantly. "Anyone says it wasn't, they're a liar!"

I was prepared to admit that maybe, just for a few seconds, it had been scary. "But not once we'd discovered what it was."

"*Rags*," said Skye. She still sounded bitter. "I told you he shouldn't have been there."

Omigod! She was still going on.

"Look, I'm sorry," I said, "it was the bread. It won't happen again. All I'm saying, there isn't any reason for nightmares when all it was was just one poor little innocent dog trying to get something to eat. OK?"

Jem pursed her lips. She was wearing her stubborn expression; the one that means she's not going to listen to a word you say.

"Could just as easily have been something else."

"But it *wasn't*."

"Still could have been."

Me and Skye exchanged glances. Skye shook her head. Jem can be just *so* illogical at times, there is no conducting any sort of rational conversation with her.

"It's very dangerous," she said, "getting in touch with spirits. You never know what's going to turn up. There's all sorts of evil out there."

I didn't quite know what to say to that. Skye muttered, "That's just a load of rubbish."

"It's not! It's not rubbish!" Jem assured us of it, earnestly. "There's good spirits and bad spirits and you meddle at your peril!"

Excuse me? This was our friend Jem speaking? Even Skye seemed a bit taken aback.

"I told Mum," said Jem, "and sh—"

"You told your mum?" I stared at her, horrified.

"I had to! She wanted to know what my nightmare was about."

"What *was* it about?" said Skye. "As a matter of interest?"

"Horrible black shapes all flapping and moaning. Mum says we're too young to hold seances; she says we'll upset ourselves."

I said, "I didn't upset myself."

"That's cos you have no imagination," said Jem.

What cheek! I have a *huge* imagination. I am always imagining things. I am just not morbid like Jem.

"Did your mum say anything else?" I said.

"Just that Angel did the right thing making me drink hot tea."

"She didn't say anything about telling my mum?"

Jem said no, but I had this uneasy feeling. Mums talk! They gossip. They bump into each other in supermarkets and stand for hours grumbling on about their children and how they've cut holes in their bedroom carpets or burned down the garden shed or gone and held seances when they'd been expressly told not to.

I sighed. I could already feel a lecture coming on.

Sure enough, Mum was waiting for me when I got home that afternoon. She said, "Jem's mum came round today."

I said, "*Oh?*"

"She wanted me to run up some curtains for her."

"Oh."

"She was telling me," said Mum, "how Jemma's

been having nightmares."

I said, "Jem's always having nightmares. She's got this really morbid streak."

"Which isn't helped by her supposedly [this is mum speaking so I reckon supposedly is OK?] best friend frightening her half to death!"

"It was Rags," I said.

"It was *you*!" said Mum. "Seriously, Frankie, I want you to promise me… no more seances. Do I have your word?"

I said yes, cos what else could I say?

"I know it just seems like a bit of fun," said Mum, "and I'm not saying there's any real harm in it, but some people do find it upsetting. *Sensitive* people," said Mum. "Like Jem. You wouldn't want to be responsible for turning her into a nervous wreck, would you?"

I agreed that I wouldn't. It was all a bit depressing. I just didn't see how Skye was ever going to find her pencil.

CHAPTER TEN

It is very hard to admit this, but if it hadn't been for Angel I might almost have given up. Me, that hates to be beaten! And *Angel*, of all people. Not that she encouraged me. She was still going on about the seance and how I was just, like, totally irresponsible and nobody in their right mind could say *she* had anything to do with it.

But then this spooky thing happened. I got up on Tuesday morning to hear Angel screeching in the bathroom. Mum came scudding up the stairs going,

"What on earth is the matter now?" I scudded after her, followed by Rags. We found Angel with her face close to the bathroom mirror, screeching as she pulled open one of her eyes and hysterically peered at it.

"What's the problem?" said Mum.

"My eye!" Angel spun round, dramatically. "Look at it!"

Me and Mum both looked. Seemed just like any ordinary sort of eye to me.

"It's red!" wailed Angel.

"Nonsense," said Mum. "A little bit pink, that's all."

"That's how it started last time!"

A few months back she'd had this infection – *minor* infection – and had to put drops in her eyes. Nobody except her would ever have noticed there was anything wrong, but she'd gone, like, way over the top and refused to leave the house for days on end. Now she was at it again.

"How can I go out with my eye like this?"

"Oh, don't be so dramatic!" said Mum. "If it makes

you any happier, we'll bathe it in salt water. For goodness' sake! Don't go *looking* for trouble."

That was when it struck me. It was one of my horoscopes: *Be on the lookout: trouble ahead.* How spooky was that???

"I just feel so guilty!" I waited till me and Jem were on our own next day, walking round the schoolyard at break. I didn't want to say anything in front of Skye.

Jem said, "Cos of Angel's eye?"

"No! There's nothing the matter with her eye, she's just a drama queen. But don't you see? It was one of my predictions! *Be on the lookout: trouble ahead.*"

Jem did this thing where she twitches her nose like a rabbit. "I don't get it," she said. "What's it got to do with Angel?"

"It's what she was doing! She was looking in the mirror… on the lookout! Convincing herself that her eye was going to go again. Plus," I added, just to make things quite plain, "it's trouble *ahead.*

Right? Your *eyes* are in your *head*!"

Jem said, "So what? Doesn't mean your horoscope was put with her star sign. It's probably just coincidence."

She'd tried saying that before. But it had to be more than just coincidence. That was the third of my predictions to come true!

"Thing is," I said, "we can't afford to just give up. Not when I might be the cause of everything. It'd be like letting Skye down."

"Mm. I s'pose," Jem admitted somewhat reluctantly. "But I don't want any more seances!"

I told her that we couldn't, anyway, cos I'd promised Mum. "But that doesn't mean we can't try something else."

"Like what?"

"I'll think of something," I said.

I thought about it all the rest of the day. I'd tried the tea leaves; I'd tried the pendulum; I'd tried the crystal ball. What *hadn't* I tried? And then, suddenly, it came to me – a Ouija board!

As soon as I'd got home and had my tea, I raced up to my room and put "Ouija boards" into the computer. From what I read, I really, honestly couldn't see there was anything for Mum to get fussed over. It wasn't like we'd actually be meeting any spirits; just asking questions and waiting for the answers to appear. All you needed was a board with numbers and letters on it, and something to use as a pointer.

I had an absolutely brilliant idea for the pointer! Just a few weeks ago I had accidentally let Rags into Mum and Dad's bedroom when I'd gone in there to use the printer, and by mistake I had knocked a load of stuff off Dad's desk, including the mouse, which Rags had immediately jumped on. By the time I got it off him, it wasn't working any more. As I said to Dad, it wasn't Rags' fault; he probably thought it was a rat. Dad agreed that Rags wasn't to blame. He seemed to think if it was anyone's fault, it was mine for letting him in there. They always say that. Everything is always my fault. I am used to it.

Anyway, I'd brought the shattered mouse back to my room for Rags to play with, except he didn't seem interested any more, now that he'd successfully killed it, so I'd chucked it in my waste bin and there it was, just waiting to be recycled. I do believe in recycling! The little wheel it ran on was still working. All I had to do was find something, like a pencil stub, maybe, and stick it on the end, and hey presto! (Magic word.) A perfect pointer!

For the board I *could* just have used sheets of paper Sellotaped together, but I like to do things properly. I waited till Dad had gone off to the DIY store, where I knew he'd be most of the afternoon (Dad just loves the DIY store!), and I waited till Mum was safely shut up in the front room with one of her ladies, where I knew she would also be most of the afternoon, cos she had this big fitting to do on bridesmaids' outfits. I didn't know where Tom was, but Tom didn't matter. What was important was that my annoying sister was also out. I could get to work with no one to spy on me!

I went down to Dad's shed (the one they accused me of setting fire to) and looked around to see what I could find. Dad has all sorts of useful and interesting stuff in his shed. There was a large cardboard box on the workbench. Empty! Exactly what I needed. It was a good box, nice and stiff. I slit it down the sides very neatly and carefully and cut round the bottom edges so that I ended up with a large rectangle. Perfect!

I took it indoors and up to my room – creeping on tiptoe along the hall, just in case – and spent the next hour lovingly decorating it. At the top, on one side, in red felt tip, I wrote the word "YES", and on the other side, "NO". I then took a black marker and wrote the letters A to M in a half-circle, and underneath, in another half-circle, N to Z. Underneath that, I put numbers, 1, 2, 3, 4, 5, 6, 7, 8, 9, 0, like it said on *Make your own Ouija Board*. As a finishing touch, down at the bottom, I wrote "Thank you", cos of needing to be polite and treating the spirits with respect.

I was quite proud of my Ouija board! I wish we did that sort of thing at school, instead of boring cooking and sewing. We did once make houses out of shoeboxes when I was at primary school, but Rags went and sat on mine and squashed it. I bet if he hadn't, it would have been one of the ones on display. I sometimes think that if I don't go for a career helping people, like giving them advice, or telling them what to do, I could have a career making things. If there *are* careers in making things. Maybe I could be an inventor. It is just a thought.

When Dad came back from the DIY shop, he brought a copy of one of the local free papers with him. Guess what I saw on the first page? An ad for Ouija board sessions!

YOUR QUESTIONS CHANNELLED THROUGH GENUINE PSYCHIC. ANSWERS GUARANTEED.

How often did that happen? It had to be an omen!

*

Excitedly, first thing Monday morning, I told Jem and Skye about it.

"On the front page... an advert! There's this woman that you go to and she asks questions for you and gets the answers."

"You're suggesting we ought to go to her?" said Skye.

"No! I'm just saying... it's an omen!"

Jem seemed doubtful. "I thought omens were bad?"

"Not if they're good ones."

"But how would you know?"

"What she means," said Skye, "is it's like a sign, saying 'Go for it!'"

"But it could be a *bad* sign."

"If it comes to that," I said, "anything could be anything."

There was a pause.

"That is so profound," said Skye.

Well, I thought it was.

Jem said, "I don't get why you're so excited."

"*Because* –" I tried not to sound too triumphant – "I've already made a Ouija board for us! It's all ready and waiting. We can ask it things whenever we like. It's just a question of where we do it. See, I'm not sure we should use my place again cos of – well, cos of Rags." I didn't want to admit that it was cos of Mum. Playing with a Ouija board mightn't be the same as holding a seance, but I sort of had this feeling she still wouldn't be too happy. Probably Jem's mum wouldn't, either, which only left Skye, and even she seemed hesitant.

She said, "I *suppose* you could come round after school. Just so long as we don't let Mum know what we're doing. She says she doesn't want me to keep on searching. She says it's making me upset and I should just try to forget about it."

That was *three* of our mums against us. Life certainly is an uphill struggle at times.

Anyway, we decided that if we were going to do it, then we should get on and *do* it. I said that next day I would bring the Ouija board into school with me – which, as it turned out, was one of those things that was easier said than done. No way would it fit into my schoolbag. I had to use a big carrier and hope Mum wouldn't ask me what I'd got in there, which fortunately she didn't, being in too much of a hurry to get rid of me so she could make a start on her bridesmaids' outfits.

Angel's beady eyes, needless to say, homed in. She said, "What's in there?" Like it was anything to do with her. I told her quite smartly that it was none of her business, whereupon she swished her hair and said, "Suit yourself! Not really interested, anyway." So why ask? She just can't *ever* stop interfering.

At break time I showed the board to Skye and Jem. They were impressed! You could tell. They gazed at it for a long time without speaking. I could see the awe on their faces. And then Skye said, "Why have you put S before R? Is that some kind of special Ouija thing?"

I must admit to being a little irritated. "It's just a small mistake," I said. I mean, really! Like it mattered. The letters were all there; who cared what order they came in?

"What's this?" said Jem, picking up the mouse.

"That's the pointer," I said.

"Why's it got a bit of old pencil stuck on it?"

"So that it can point!"

"I thought with a Ouija board you used a tumbler," said Skye.

"Well, we're using a mouse!" It was *my* board; it was *my* idea. "If you think you can do any better…"

"You don't have to get all huffed up," said Skye. "I was only asking."

I was about to put the board back in its carrier bag when Daisy Hooper came clumping past.

"Ooh, is that a Weejy board?" she said. "We played with one of those at Christmas. My gran got a message from a girl she was at school with. She didn't even know she'd died! Dead scary."

There are times when I could happily *throttle*

Daisy Hooper. Opening her big mouth. It was all we needed! Jem plucked anxiously at my sleeve as we went back into school.

"I don't want to do it if it's going to be scary!"

"It's not," I said soothingly. "There's nothing to be frightened of. We're just going to ask questions. *I'm* going to ask questions." I paused. "Cos of me being the one that's read about it. Plus," I added carelessly, "me being the one that's most likely psychic."

I waited for Jem to start up about the huge hairy monsters racing across her kitchen floor, and how it was exactly what she'd written in her horoscope, but it seemed she wasn't interested any more in having psychic powers cos she just chewed her bottom lip and didn't say anything.

"You are still coming, aren't you?" I whispered as the bell rang for the end of afternoon school.

I half expected her to find some excuse, like she'd suddenly remembered she'd got to be home early, or she had a dentist appointment, but one thing we always do, we always stick by one another. Jem said she'd already told her mum she'd be late home.

"Only not *too* late."

Me and Skye agreed, not *too* late. We told her that she was being very brave.

"I wouldn't do it for just anyone," said Jem, sounding rather pitiful.

I said, "Of course you wouldn't! It's the sort of thing you only do for your friends. But honestly, it won't be like last time. I mean, for one thing, we're doing it in daylight."

"Yes, and it's only questions and answers," said Skye. "Nothing spooky."

"There won't be any dead people?"

Patiently I explained that all the dead people were "up there".

"So how do they answer questions?"

"Well, it's like this sort of… *energy*. Psychic energy. Flowing down." I dabbled my fingers in the air, to show the energy rippling through space. "What it'll do, it'll flow down my arm and into my hand, and that's what'll make the mouse move."

"What about *our* hands?" said Skye. "Where are they going to be?"

"On the mouse! Everybody puts their fingers on it."

"Do we have to?" said Jem. "Couldn't I just sit and watch?"

Skye looked at me doubtfully. "Would it work with just two of us?"

I didn't see why not. "Might even work better," I said, "cos then we'd have someone to write down the messages. Save us having to keep breaking off. Jem can be our secretary! Special Ouija secretary."

Jem liked that idea. I guess it made her feel that she was playing her part without actually having to come into contact with any dead people.

We got to Skye's house to find that neither her mum nor her dad had arrived back from work, which I couldn't help feeling was a good sign. Another omen! Nobody there to ask questions, nobody to come bursting in on us.

"Let's go straight upstairs and get on with it,"

id Skye. She meant before her mum got back.

Skye's bedroom has buttercup-yellow walls and bright green rugs and is very *neat* and *clean* and *tidy*. Not, to my way of thinking, the ideal place to consult a Ouija board. I said as much to Skye. I wasn't being critical or anything, but spirits do like a bit of atmosphere. A bit of gloom and shadow. That's all I was saying! She didn't have to take offence.

I *know* my bedroom gets into a mess, I *know* I don't clean it up as often as I'm supposed to, I *know* that sometimes there are even cobwebs dangling from the lampshade, but that's because Mum says she's too busy to do proper mum-type things like housework. What she calls "running about after you".

I pointed this out to Skye, but all she did was sniff and say she was sorry if her room wasn't messy enough.

"It's just that it would be better," I said, "if it was a bit dark. Like if we could pull the curtains and have candles? Spirits don't really respond too well to daylight."

There was an immediate squeal from Jem. "I'm not doing it in the dark!"

"Nobody is doing it in the dark," said Skye. "Stop making excuses! I thought you were supposed to have all this massive psychic power?"

"I just don't want you to be disappointed," I said. "Maybe the spirits will speak, maybe they won't. We can but try."

"Yeah, right," said Skye. "Where are the questions?"

We'd already made a list, starting off with simple ones that just required a *yes* or a *no*.

"Until we see whether it's a friendly spirit or an— Ow, ouch!" I rubbed reproachfully at my ankle. Skye, out of sight of Jem, pulled a hideous face. "That is," I gabbled, "a spirit that wants to help, cos I mean they'll all be *friendly*. Obviously!" I gave a little reassuring laugh. "It's just that some mightn't actually know anything; they might just be kind of curious, or—"

"Why don't we try *asking* them?" said Skye.

We put the Ouija board on Skye's desk, with me and Skye sitting opposite one another, our fingers on the mouse, and Jem cross-legged on the bed, where she could feel safe with a pen and a notebook.

I said, "OK! Question number one…" I closed my eyes and concentrated. "Is anybody there? Please answer!"

The mouse zipped off into the top left-hand corner. *YES!*

"Is it convenient for you to speak to us?"

YES.

"Are you Skye's gran?"

We all held our breath. The mouse skittered in a circle. *NO.*

"Do you know Skye's gran?"

The mouse shuttled uncertainly from one side of the board to the other. *YES. NO. YES. NO.*

I said, "Please tell us if you know Skye's gran!"

NO.

Skye let out her breath.

"Is that it?" said Jem.

I said, "No, we've hardly started!" Trust Jem to go and interrupt when I was getting on so well – the first time I'd found a spirit that was willing to talk!

"Ask if it can do anything to help," said Skye.

"OK." I put on my best voice. My polite voice. The one I use for one of my grans, who is always urging us to "speak properly". "If it is not too much trouble, o friendly spirit, I wonder if you could go and have a look and see if you can find Skye's gran for us? Her name," I added, "is Mrs Samuels."

We waited, but nothing happened. The mouse wobbled a bit, but didn't seem to want to go anywhere.

"Tell it we'd be most grateful," hissed Skye.

"We would be most grateful," I said. "Oh, and if you find her, could you possibly ask her, do you think, if she knows where the silver pencil is that she left Skye in her will?"

There was a pause while the spirit obviously thought about things. For a moment the mouse just stayed where it was, not moving, but then, with a sudden spurt, went skittering across to the top left-hand corner. *YES!*

I turned triumphantly to Jem. "It's going to go and look!"

"How long d'you think it'll take?"

"Dunno."

"Can't you ask it?"

I said, "No! That'd be rude."

Jem wriggled. "I want to go to the loo!"

"Well, you can't," said Skye. "That would be very bad manners. You'll just have to hold on to it."

"I can't!"

I said, "Oh, all *right*. But if it gets upset, don't blame me." I put on my polite voice again; very humble, cos it did seem a bit of an impertinence. "I don't mean to push you or anything, o spirit, but can you let us know how long it might take?"

In what seemed like a bit of a huff, the mouse

went trundling off up the board. It beetled about among the numbers for a few seconds, then finally plonked itself down on number three.

"Does that mean three minutes?" I said. "Excuse me for asking, it's just that we have to go home soon."

The spirit didn't like that. Maybe I shouldn't have asked. The mouse set off at an angry gallop towards the right-hand corner. *NO.* My heart sank. If it wasn't three minutes, did that mean it was three hours? Three days? *Longer?* But then – oh, joy! – it suddenly changed its mind and took a run in the opposite direction. Three minutes!

"Thank you *sooo* much," I said.

I sank back, feeling quite exhausted. It is a strain, having to watch what you're saying all the time, and how you're saying it. Like talking to the Queen. Jem had started on again about going to the loo, but I shushed her.

"No talking!" Especially about *that.* "It'll disturb them."

Jem sank down, muttering, while me and Skye kept our eyes glued to the second hand on Skye's alarm clock. It seemed like for ever, but we didn't dare move for fear of bad manners. Spirits can be very touchy if they feel you're dissing them. Jem was shifting about on the bed, huffing and puffing to herself, but as she was outside the actual circle I was hoping the spirits wouldn't take any notice.

As soon as the three minutes were up, me and Skye placed our fingers back on the mouse and I asked the all-important question. "Welcome back, o spirit! Have you been able to find out where the pencil is?"

The mouse immediately went racing up to the left-hand corner: *YES*.

"Please can you tell us?"

YES.

I flapped at Jem with my free hand. "Pay attention!"

"I am paying attention! I'm—"

"Sh!"

The mouse turned in a circle and headed up the board. Skye sang out the letters as it flitted to and fro: "D – B – E – oops!"

She gave a little cry of alarm as it suddenly spun out of control, tearing from letter to letter at breakneck speed, so fast we could hardly keep up with it.

"R – E – R – H – A – W – A – O – R," gabbled Skye.

At which point the mouse shot away from us and went skittering straight off the board.

We sat back, startled.

I turned anxiously to Jem. "Did you get all that?"

"I think so," said Jem.

"I hope you did," I said, "cos we can't ask it to repeat itself." The thing with Jem, she's not always totally reliable. She means well, but she has a mind that *flits*.

"What's it say?" demanded Skye.

"Doesn't say anything."

"It's got to say *something*. Read it out!"

Jem cleared her throat.

"DBERERHAWAOR."

With an impatient click of the tongue, Skye reached over and whisked the notebook away from her. She studied it, frowning.

"D'berer ha waor!"

There was a silence.

"What is it supposed to mean?" wondered Jem.

CHAPTER
ELEVEN

We all agreed that that was the question: what did it mean?

"It must mean *something*," I said. "Why send a message if it doesn't mean anything?"

Jem suggested that it might be a secret code, but what would be the point of that? It had come from Skye's gran! Why would she use a secret code?

"Could just be the way they talk," said Jem. "A sort of special spirit language so's they can all understand each other."

"Mm…." We considered the idea. Jem does just occasionally have a flash of inspiration.

"Let's Google it," said Skye.

We tried Googling it in one long string, and we tried Googling it in little bits, but nothing came up.

This is what I mean about computers. Sometimes they can be quite clever; other times they are just *ignorant*.

"If they can translate Chinese," said Jem, "you'd think they could translate a bit of spirit language."

"If that's what it is," said Skye.

"What else could it be?"

We all waited for someone to make a suggestion, but nobody did. I guess none of us wanted to admit that the message might not be a message at all, but just a load of nonsense.

After a bit, Jem slid herself off the bed and said apologetically that she probably ought to be getting home now.

"I mean… we're not doing it again. Right?"

Skye sighed and said, "I suppose not." I didn't

contradict her. Even I was beginning to lose heart. I'd gone to all that trouble! Making a Ouija board, finding out how to use it, risking life and limb smuggling it out of the house under Mum's nose. And for what? A rubbishing kind of message that nobody could understand.

Jem and I walked home together in glum silence. Jem is almost *never* silent. I am not very often silent myself, if it comes to that. We reached Jem's road and stood for a moment, hesitating.

Jem said, "Well…"

There was a pause. Then I said, "Well…"

"See you tomorrow," said Jem.

I said, "Yeah. See you tomorrow."

Mum was in the kitchen when I arrived home.

"Still lugging that carrier bag?" she said. "What on earth have you got in there?"

"Nothing," I said. I clutched at it defensively. "Just something for school."

"All right, you don't have to be so prickly! What's

your problem?"

"Haven't got a problem."

"So why are you all humpish?"

I opened my mouth to say that I wasn't all humpish, but sometimes I find it helps to talk to Mum. Just so long as she didn't keep on about the carrier bag.

"It's Skye," I said. "We've been trying to help her find her gran's pencil, but now her mum says she's got to stop looking cos it's upsetting her. She says it's time to give up. Just move on and forget about it. But how can she? It's like asking her to forget her gran!"

I waited for Mum to say that she agreed with me. But she didn't.

She said that although it was very sad, she reckoned Skye's mum was probably right.

"Forgetting about the pencil isn't the same as forgetting her gran. You don't ever forget the people you love."

It wasn't what I wanted to hear! I wanted Mum

to tell me that we shouldn't give up. But I might have known she'd side with Mrs Solomons. Mums always stick together.

I trailed up to my room, munching half-heartedly on an apple. I don't really care for apples. I'd only taken it cos it was there and I couldn't be bothered to look for anything else. I felt like my old teddy bear must have felt when Rags chewed a hole in him and pulled out all his stuffing. All limp and empty. I had *so* wanted to find Skye's pencil for her!

I gave the apple core to Rags to finish off and wondered what to do with my beautiful Ouija board. I couldn't bring myself to throw it away, so I put it in the bottom of my wardrobe, propped up at the back behind some trainers. I didn't really see that Mum would have any reason to look in there, but even if she did she probably wouldn't notice. I mean, for a start, it's pretty dark inside a wardrobe, and Mum likes to get in and out of my room double quick cos she says it disturbs her. It makes her want to come in and clean up, which I tell her she is very welcome to do, but it seems that she can't, apparently. It is some weird kind of principle. However, just to be on the safe side I turned the board back to front so that all she would see was a label saying E.J. TOOLS LTD, WOLVERHAMPTON.

I suppose I had this thought in my mind that maybe, one day, when Jem was feeling a bit braver, we might have another go. I really do *hate* to give up.

Dad came in at half past five and Mum called me to come and have some tea. Angel was already there, chewing on a stick of celery, with a dish of shredded carrot and a pot of low-fat yogurt. This is her idea of a good meal. She is totally mad. Tom, as usual, was plugged into his iPod, mindlessly shovelling spaghetti hoops into his mouth. Tom eats anything that is put before him, he doesn't even notice. I reckon he'd be just as happy with a bowl of earthworms.

"Where's Dad?" I said.

"Gone out to the shed to look for something.

Don't ask," said Mum. "He's had a bad day. His drill's broken."

"His new one?" I said. "He only got it last week!"

"I know." Mum pulled a face. "He's not best pleased. He's going to have to send it back."

I said, "Poor Dad! He loves his tools."

"He loves them even better when they work," said Mum. "Sh!" She put a finger to her lips. "Here he comes. Whatever you do, don't mention the drill!" She turned with a bright smile as Dad appeared at the back door. "Everything all right?"

Dad said, "No, everything is not all right! Would you believe it, I can't find the box?"

"Oh dear," said Mum. "Don't you have another one?"

"I don't want another one! I want the one it came in."

"So." Mum spoke very slowly and carefully. "What do you think you could have done with it?"

"I know exactly what I did with it! I left it in the shed."

"In the shed. Right." Mum nodded. "There is quite a lot of stuff in that shed. Have you tried I—"

"On my workbench!" roared Dad. "I left it on my workbench!" He spun round, glaring at us. "Who's been there? Who's been in my shed?"

Angel, crunching celery, hunched her shoulders up to her ears. Tom said, "What?" I didn't say anything. I have this belief that in moments of crisis it is essential not to panic. If I prayed hard enough, maybe a miracle might occur.

And, oh, one did! The telephone rang and Dad had to go rushing out.

"It's the old boy up the road," he said. "Some sort of emergency. I won't be long, he's probably just blown a fuse."

Well! I felt sorry for Dad, having to miss his tea, but it quite restored my faith in the power of prayer. Miracles *can* happen!

By the time Dad got back he seemed to have forgotten about his missing box, he just wanted to settle down and relax. A narrow escape, if ever there was!

I wondered if I ought to feel guilty. It wasn't like I'd done anything wrong! Just cutting up an old cardboard box. How was I to know it was the box Dad's drill had come in? How was I to know the drill was going to be faulty and have to be sent back? It was the drill company that was to blame, not me! I'd just been trying to help Skye.

Jem and I were really surprised, next morning, to find Skye waiting for us in our usual spot with this huge great beam on her face. Skye is not at all a beaming sort of person. Plus, in any case, what could she possibly have to beam about? I'd been rehearsing what to say to her. I didn't think, necessarily, that I needed to grovel. I mean, it was hardly my fault if the spirits chose to send silly coded messages that didn't make any sense; I couldn't be held responsible for the way they behaved. On the other hand, I did feel sorry that things hadn't worked out.

I was just about to open my mouth and say so when Skye got in ahead of me.

"D'berer," she cried, "ha waor!"

Omigod. She'd flipped.

"D'berer." She flashed us this bright smile. "Ha waor!"

Rather nervously, Jem said, "Absolutely. I couldn't agree more. You're so right!" Then spinning round so that her back was turned on Skye, she hissed, "What is she talking about?"

"Anagrams!" Skye announced it triumphantly. "It was an anagram!"

Jem said, "Nanagram?"

Even I knew better than that. I said, "*Anagram*. It's where you jiggle letters around."

"Exactly," said Skye. "I've been jiggling and jiggling! I kept waking up in the night, almost driving myself mad, and then this morning… ta-da!" With a flourish, she produced something from out of her pocket. Something small and slim and silvery. "It came to me!"

"*Oh.*" Jem clapped a hand to her mouth. "You found it!"

Her gran's pencil!

"Where?" I said. "Where?"

"In Gran's room," Skye giggled. "It was there all along!"

"But how did you find it?"

"I worked out the anagram. *D'berer ha waor…* If you jiggle the letters around they spell WARDROBE. *Er ha wardrobe.*"

Jem crinkled her nose. "What's *er ha* mean?"

"It's like when someone's speaking," said Skye. "Like, er – ha – *wardrobe!*"

"And that's where you found it?" I couldn't help shooting this little sly glance at Jem. *Now* let her say I wasn't psychic! "Right there, in the wardrobe?"

"Oh, it wasn't in the *wardrobe*," said Skye. "I'd already looked in there heaps of times."

I was getting a bit lost. "So where was it, then?"

"It had fallen into this tiny little crack between the wall and the edge of the carpet. We only didn't see it before cos of the chest of drawers being there."

Jem's chest went puffing out. "So it wasn't anything to do with the Ouija board!"

"Excuse me," I said. "If it hadn't been for the Ouija board, she wouldn't ever have thought to go back and have another look."

Skye agreed that she probably wouldn't. "I'd just about given up, you know? If it hadn't been for you guys, I would have done! It was only when I worked out the message I felt I had to have one last go."

"But the message got it wrong," protested Jem. "It didn't mean anything!"

"That's all you know," I said. "You can't expect spirits to talk in ordinary everyday language. You have to be able to interpret what they're saying. I mean, fr'instance, if Skye's gran couldn't actually remember where she'd left the pencil, which she probably couldn't, she might well have said 'er ha wardrobe' meaning *Have another look!*'."

Jem did that thing that she does, crinkling her

nose. She just didn't want to believe, even now, that I was the one who was psychic.

"Why don't we check out our horoscope pages?" I said. That would show her! "I know you said not till the end of term, but we've only got a few days to go, and—"

"You can check them out, if you like," said Skye. "They're still in my bag; I'd forgotten all about them."

"Let's do it at break," I said. "We can read them all out and see who got the most right."

I'd thought it would be fun, but Skye and Jem both seemed to have lost interest. Skye had never been all that interested to begin with, but even Jem no longer seemed to care whether any of the things she'd predicted had actually come true. Just as well, since none of them had! She did try mumbling about the one that I'd picked. *Things will happen.* But she only did it half-heartedly. She didn't argue when Skye pointed out that things are always happening.

"Especially to Frankie!"

"But look," I said, "look what I wrote for Virgo…
An exciting new opportunity will arise. Virgo's my
mum's star sign, and guess what?"

There was a silence. Then Jem said, "What?"

"She did have an exciting opportunity! She was
offered a month's free trial at a gym."

Very solemnly, Skye said, "Wow."

I could tell they weren't impressed, but I was!
How often do you get offered a month's free trial?
A whole month without having to pay for it!

"What about Skye's one?" said Jem. "*Trouble
ahead.* That didn't happen! That was one of yours.
Now, if she'd had *this* one –" Jem jabbed a finger
– "*A treasured possession will be lost.* That'd make
more sense."

I have to admit, that was the one I thought she'd
picked. But the other one was just as good. After
all, there had been trouble. Skye had got a B– for
her maths homework. That was trouble big time!

"If you ask me," said Jem, "it's a load of nonsense."
She swept up all the bits of paper and scrunched

them into a ball. "You'd have to be really stupid to believe any of it."

Really, there are times Jem quite takes my breath away.

"What about your auntie?" I said. "All that stuff with the tomato ketchup."

"Oh, that!" Jem dismissed it with a wave of the hand. Like she hadn't gone on and on and on about it. "Mum says Auntie Fay talks a lot of rubbish."

Now she told us.

"Well, anyway," I said, "it was my Ouija board helped Skye find her pencil."

"Yes, it was," said Skye. She suddenly threw her arms round me and hugged me. I was, like, knocked out! Skye just doesn't do that kind of thing. "You can copy my maths homework any time you want," she said. "Both of you! And I won't have a go at either of you ever again, about anything, *ever*."

She would, of course. She wouldn't be Skye if she wasn't always lecturing us and telling us off. But that was all right. She was our friend, and you have to accept your friends the way they are.

I could hardly wait to get home that afternoon and tell Mum. Not about the Ouija board, of course, but about Skye. I knew she'd be pleased.

"Mum," I said, bursting through the kitchen door, "Skye found her p—"

I stopped. There on the kitchen table was my Ouija board.

"Ah, you're back," said Mum. "I've been waiting for you to arrive. What, pray, is this?"

How had she found it? What had she been doing in my wardrobe?

"It's – um – ah – a sort of game," I said. "A sort of… asking questions sort of thing. It's not the same as a seance! I was just trying to h—"

"I meant," said Mum, "what is *this*? E.J. TOOLS LTD?"

I swallowed.

"It's your dad's box! The one he was looking for."

Wild thoughts whizzed at supersonic speed

round my head. It wasn't Dad's box, it was a totally different box! It was a box I'd found on the pavement, I'd brought home from school, it had already been cut up, someone else must have done it, it wasn't me, it wasn't—

"Well?" said Mum.

"I can explain!" I said.

"I think you'd better," said Mum. "Your dad's in the other room. I suggest you go and throw yourself on his mercy."

Dad was lying back on the sofa, watching television. He looked tired. He'd been getting up really early just lately, like four o'clock in the morning. I wished I had something nice to tell him instead of having to make a horrible confession.

"Um… Dad," I said.

"Mm?"

I took a deep breath.

"I'm-very-sorry-to-have-to-announce-that-it-was-me-that-cut-up-your-box." The words came gabbling out. I knew it wasn't any use waiting for another miracle. There are times when you just have to be brave and go for it.

"I didn't mean to cut it up! I didn't know you wanted it. I wouldn't have done it if I'd known you wanted it! I thought it was just an empty box. I mean, it was an empty box! I didn't know your drill had come in it. I just wanted something to make a Ouija board, which is not the same thing as a seance, I wouldn't have held another seance cos Mum told me not to, and I promised I wouldn't, but she didn't say anything about Ouija boards! It was for Skye, cos of her gran dying and Skye not being able to find her silver pencil, and she was so unhappy! I just wanted to help her, and I did help her, cos you'll never guess what… she's found the pencil and it's all because of me! And cos of your box, which I'm very very sorry about, but—"

"Fifty lashes," said Dad, "and no pocket money for the next six months."

I stared.

"Oh, go away, go away!" Dad waved a hand. "I've

solved the problem. Just don't destroy any more boxes without asking me."

Phew! I turned and fled, crashing into Angel, busy eavesdropping at the door.

"So it was you," she hissed. "I might have known it!"

I shoved past her. "You'd better watch it," I said. "I have psychic powers!" I rushed back to the kitchen exultantly. "Mum, I—"

"Did you tell him?"

"Yes, and Mum—"

"Did you apologise?"

"Yes! Mum, listen… Skye found her pencil! *I* found her pencil. It was in her gran's room all the time, and it was all thanks to me!" I grabbed Rags by his front paws and we danced together round the kitchen. "I found the pencil, I found the pencil!"

I guess it must have been Rags' tail that swept the milk off the table. Accidents happen! Mum didn't have to get all tetchy about it.

"Frankie Foster," she said, "you just clean that up!

I'm not getting down there with my back. And make sure you don't leave the floor like a skating rink this time. It's thanks to you I have a bad back in the first place!"

I couldn't help reflecting that if Mum had gone to the gym when the opportunity was there, she wouldn't still have a bad back. That is what gyms are for, to sort out these things. I did tell her! If only people would just *listen* to me occasionally. But they never do. They are too busy blaming me for everything.

"And *please*," said Mum, "*don't* splosh water about like that! Use some kitchen roll."

There she went again. Poor Mum! She gets so worked up.

"See, look, now I'm using kitchen roll," I said. "All nice and dry!"

"Thank you," said Mum, cracking eggs into a bowl. "I appreciate that."

I suppose, really, it is quite easy to make her happy. I'd made Skye happy, too! And Dad had solved his problems, and Jem had accepted that she didn't have any psychic powers, which I'd known all along she hadn't, and next week was half term, so yay! I squished the kitchen roll into a ball and tossed it to Rags, who skidded across the floor and—

Oops!

Mum stood, gazing in silent wonderment at the spreading puddle of egg.

"Do you know what?" she said. "I'm going to go and sit down."

"That's right," I said. "You take it easy. No problem! I'll sort things out."

But I didn't have to. Rags was already seeing to it.

"Look at that," I said. "He's cleaned it all up for you!"

And guess what?

The floor was bone dry.

"Funny, funky, feisty — and fantastic reads!" *JACQUELINE WILSON*

FRANKIE FOSTER

Pick 'n' Mix

Here to Help!

Jean Ure

Jean Ure

PUMPKIN PIE

"Funny, funky, feisty – and fantastic reads!"
Jacqueline Wilson

Coming Soon!